"*Love War Stories* serves up love every which way: thwarted, obsessive, suffered over, delirious, consummated, unexpected. It rejects cultural traditions yet remains beholden to them. It fights with itself and others. It worships Julia de Burgos (as do I). And at its best, it is sublime. Brava to Ivelisse Rodriguez for a stunning debut!"

—CRISTINA GARCÍA, author of
Dreaming in Cuban

"This is the short story collection I've been waiting for. *Love War Stories* arrests the heart with its stunning exploration of women who are put through a kind of hell in their determination to find true love. Hilarious at times even in the midst of the tragic and heartbreaking, *Love War Stories* is extraordinary—punto y final."

—ANGIE CRUZ, author of *Let It Rain Coffee*

"Wise, ferocious, and beautifully executed, these tales trace the tangled roots of trauma and desire. Ivelisse Rodriguez is a writer to watch, and *Love War Stories* is a thrilling debut."

—PATRICIA ENGEL, author of
The Veins of the Ocean

"A tough smart dazzling debut by a tough smart dazzling writer. Ivelisse Rodriguez is a revelation."

—JUNOT DÍAZ, author of
This Is How You Lose Her

NO LONGER PROPERTY OF SEATTLE PUBLIC LIBRARY

D0391394

"An insightful look into girlhood, race, and the wounds of growing up, *Love War Stories* is a searing collection of stories. Ivelisse Rodriguez has a rare gift for describing the minutiae of contemporary life, the heartaches as well as the dangers, without flinching. A dazzling work by an important new voice."

—MARK HABER, Brazos Bookstore

LOVE
WAR
STORIES

IVELISSE RODRIGUEZ

FEMINIST
PRESS
AT THE CITY UNIVERSITY
OF NEW YORK
NEW YORK CITY

Published in 2018 by the Feminist Press
at the City University of New York
The Graduate Center
365 Fifth Avenue, Suite 5406
New York, NY 10016

feministpress.org

First Feminist Press edition 2018

Copyright © 2018 by Ivelisse Rodriguez

All rights reserved.

  This book was made possible thanks to a grant from New
York State Council on the Arts with the support of Governor
Andrew M. Cuomo and the New York State Legislature.

This book is supported in part by an award from the National Endow-
ment for the Arts.

No part of this book may be reproduced, used, or stored in any information
retrieval system or transmitted in any form or by any means, electronic, mechanical, photocopying, recording, or otherwise, without prior written permission
from the Feminist Press at the City University of New York, except in the case
of brief quotations embodied in critical articles and reviews.

First printing July 2018

Cover and text design by Suki Boynton

Library of Congress Cataloging-in-Publication Data

Names: Rodriguez, Ivelisse, author.
Title: Love war stories / Ivelisse Rodriguez.
Description: New York : Feminist Press, [2018]
Identifiers: LCCN 2017049761 (print) | LCCN 2018000050 (ebook) | ISBN
   9781936932283 (e-book) | ISBN 9781936932252 (trade pbk.)
Subjects: LCSH: Girls--Puerto Rico--Fiction.
Classification: LCC PS3618.O35825 (ebook) | LCC PS3618.O35825 A6 2018
(print)
   | DDC 813/.6--dc23
LC record available at https://lccn.loc.gov/2017049761

For Holyoke girls

CONTENTS

LOVE
WAR
STORIES

EL QUÉ DIRÁN

You belong to your husband, your master; not me;
I belong to nobody, or all . . .

You in yourself have no say; everyone governs you;
your husband, your parents, your family,
the priest, the dressmaker . . .

Not in me, in me only my heart governs,
only my thought; who governs in me is me.

—JULIA DE BURGOS, "To Julia de Burgos"

"She still waits," they joked—men sitting around a bar who, perhaps, never had to wait for anything, who saw women as handkerchiefs they carried in their back pockets, their initials stenciled into the fine lace. When Lola made her appearances outside of the house, they did not wait until she passed by to erupt. She was the observed of their keen eyes; her waiting more legendary than their love affairs.

♥

She didn't fall from the sky, but Tía Lola was the woman on the ground. Her wailing outside my window pulled me out of sleep, eclipsing the clanging of the cowbells—a sound I had become used to over the past fourteen years. Glancing down at Tía Lola, my first thought was that something must've happened with Tío Carlos. Perhaps he was dead, or worse: the letter the whole town had been waiting for, the one stating he would never return, had finally arrived.

My bare feet slapped against the kitchen floor, and I had to hold on to the doorknob as I slipped rushing outside. I didn't feel the concrete of our porch or the cold grass on the soles of my feet, or the morning dew seeping into my nightgown when I fell to my knees.

She clutched nothing new in her hands. No letter, no photo, no fresh accoutrement of hope or rejection—only the old yellowed letters. And the way her body undulated, I knew it was all the memories.

I had always wondered how long the heart could stop and start before breaking.

"Tía, what is it?" I asked.

Not even glancing at me, Tía Lola mumbled about how she met Tío Carlos at her quinceañera and repeated things I already knew. "Did you ever think he would come back?" she asked. She said all this as if she were talking to another Lola—one above her. I stroked her hair to assure her of my presence and held back my tears so hers could flow.

My back stiffened when I heard the door open and realized how I must look without a robe on to any passerby in the street. My long nightgown immediately felt too short, too sheer.

"Noelia, go inside and get dressed. I'll take care of Lola," my mother said.

Thankfully, that was all she said. The closer to my quinceañera, the more my mother loomed over me, huge wings spreading in a small nest. My mother feared that Tía Lola's misfortune would somehow rub off on me, and my mother couldn't, wouldn't, imagine another woman without a husband in this house.

I quickly whispered in my aunt's ear, "Don't worry, Tía, he'll come back."

♥

He said he would come back. It was a common practice, nothing for her to worry about. They drove all the way to San Juan because that was the only airport then. Lola cried, laughed, held his hand, kissed it, and said, "Te espero. Para siempre." She touched her stomach and corrected herself, "We'll wait." It was a year after Lola and Carlos had married. He left to make a better life for them in the United States, and before he boarded the plane with a flurry of kisses, waves, and promises he said, "Lolita, I'll make you proud. By the time I come back, your father won't have anything to say about me, about us." For seven years, the letters came and every time one arrived, Lola held it up as a beacon of his love. She ignored the tales of Carlos's life over there from those who returned without finding their fortune.

When she sat on the veranda and saw the dapper young men court her neighbor Celi, when she saw the Plymouth Roadking he once dreamed of owning, or when she saw the high-class ladies with their pearls, she thought only of Carlos. She told herself it was okay that he couldn't make it for their son Julio's birth and death,

3

that she must live with her sister, that the neighbors wove tales behind her back, and that he promised and promised but never kept because in the world Lola configured, her waiting ceased.

2,555 days stacked. Finding movement everywhere. Lola could see him, reenvision him from a smell, a touch. Carlos, so memorable in his absence.

♥

On the surface, the memories acted themselves out in Tía Lola's room. Always whiffs of perfumes, scents of last meals, laughter over love letters. The room, pregnant, was always ready to burst. The letters, normally bound, in order by date, by year, were scattered on the floor. They inhabited a white box overlaid with gold, its lid always slightly askew. Lovingly wrapped around the cluster of letters, a ribbon for each year. The red ribbon was for year two. Pink ribbon for year five. Year three: blue.

In Tía Lola's room, sheer curtains were tied back so you could access the smolder of the moon or the sun. There was always something from the outside that could be captured in this room, something always welcomed. She had a decorative mosquito net—interlocking swans embraced—she had sewn herself. Perfumes that looked like they were contained in handmade bottles lined her dresser. The room, as I will always remember it, was candlelit for moments ready to be captured and memorialized. But the centerpiece was always that box, with accumulated letters spilling out.

Tía Lola sat in her window seat. Already she seemed

different from that morning. She looked like she had cried out each hurt, each tear. Her hair was neatly down, and she had a dress she had often been photographed in—a white halter dress tied at her waist.

I tiptoed to Tía Lola's bed, near the strewn letters. "I was worried about you all day," I whispered. "How . . . do you feel? Did you hear something?"

She shook her head. "There was nothing new to hear," she mumbled. She wrapped her arms around her legs and put her head on her knees.

Just yesterday, I was so excited because we were able to bring my quinceañera dress home, and it was exactly how I had imagined it for the past three years. When everyone went to sleep last night, I sat with it, touching the glimmering rhinestones on the full-bodied tulle skirt. Slipping it on, I practiced the dance I would do in a few weeks. The material making a musical *swish-swish* sound while I counted my steps and held my arms out to an imaginary man.

Tía Lola's dress was pulled up; I could see her legs. She used to tell me how beautiful they were—her asset, besides her pretty face. But tonight, they looked thin. I saw the wear on them, like they had walked for too long. She absentmindedly rubbed them while we talked.

"Doña Santa's husband came back," I chirped.

She gave me a faint smile. "And what was he like after all those years?"

In the novela *El qué dirán*, which we had watched every afternoon for the past few months, Santa Dávila was like Tía Lola—she waited and waited. And just today, José Dávila had returned, smile broader than their distance.

5

"He was even more handsome than when he left, and he loved her even more." I picked up the most worn letter near my foot. The letters from the early years—those were my favorite. I imagined that Tía Lola lay on those letters to surround herself with his love, even today.

I filled the heavy air with his words:

Cariño, the world moves so fast here. The factory job Ignacio helped me get has been long and tiring. But I save money from each paycheck. As exhausting as it is, I wish I could get two jobs so that I could come home to you faster. I won't let you down. What you've heard isn't true, I don't have time to do much besides have one drink a week. I work and sleep. We'll have the great life we should have. I'm sorry this is what our second year of marriage looks like. I would rather be home kissing your face. I have to cut this letter short. I'm exhausted from all this work. Tomorrow I said I would fix the furnace for the landlord. He said he would give me a discount on the rent. Let's count the months and maybe this time next year this will all seem like a long-ago memory.

"He never loves you less," I said, placing the letter back with the others.

♥

The first time Lola fully immersed herself in her suffering was right after Julio came into the world stillborn. Carlos said that he would be there for months and weeks. And when her water broke, Lola tried to hold it in, to give him more time to arrive. Right before she went into labor, it flickered through her mind that he would not come.

The day after she was released from the hospital, Lola marched over to Carlos's parents' house to confront them and has not suffered in silence since. Passersby heard her shrieks and that was the first day the townsmen began their snickering. And it was the last day the women she had come to love—the ones also waiting for husbands—grieved with her. They promulgated and led the worst jeers about Lola.

Since then they have not stopped, but that does not matter to Lola, it has never mattered. The only thing that mattered was Carlos's return.

♥

To avoid explaining Tía Lola's behavior, my mother declined to go to church but ordered me and my father to go regardless because after the services, we would rehearse the quinceañera mass with the priest. At least at the church, there would be a sense of tranquility. No threats. I had woken up for eleven days to the noise of Tía Lola, and then that of my mother.

My father and I rarely spent time alone together, but for the months leading up to my quinceañera reception, we continually rehearsed our waltz. Because of that I have come to see the man my mother must see. Perpetually elegant—his hair normally parted and coiffed to the side, all his suits bought in the capital from the same stores the Americans shopped—wealth shimmering off of him.

I would invariably take a step in the wrong direction. "Don't worry, Noelia, you'll dance beautifully soon enough." A man with a calming presence. Without him, my mother would have come undone over Tía Lola's spectacle. For the first time, I felt like his daughter. His. In our house, he stood behind my mother and my mother only. Not because he was a weak man, but because she was his wife, first and foremost. My mother had always had my father, and I had always had Tía Lola.

Doña Olga, Ricardo's mother, was the first person we encountered when my father and I arrived at the mass. Ricardo was my partner in my quinceañera and, hopefully, soon in life. My father quickly acknowledged her presence. Behind my father, I peeked at Doña Olga's face to determine if she had heard about Tía Lola's wailing. She asked about my mother and then simply smiled at me, and I knew I had been dismissed. Doña Olga had never been kind to me, nor outright cruel. My mother suspected that she found me unsuitable for Ricardo because of Tía Lola, but tolerated our pairing because we are an established family. I had even overheard my mother talking about Don Andres, Ricardo's father, being in financial trouble because of drinking and gambling. Sometimes my mother thought we had the upper hand, sometimes she thought Ricardo's family did.

As soon as the mass was over, I rushed to the damas. All of us girls sat clumped together and talked among ourselves. What we were really doing, though, was conversing so that every now and then we could consider the boys who sat in the pews across from us. Even if they had never met before we started preparing for this quinceañera, each girl had taken to fantasizing about her partner. Alisa pined for Jose; Rita gazed at Luis; Yvette pouted at Pedro . . . All fifteen of us girls took turns dreaming.

Ricardo. Each time, I was struck by his beauty—dark wavy hair and dimples. Broad-shouldered and a self-satisfied smile. Other girls said he reminded them so much of the new American movie star Marlon Brando. I had even caught older women flirting with or gawking at my Ricardo. All our lives we had lived across from each other, and all my life I had known that one day we would be here. If any of these girls in my quinceañera could change escorts, they would choose him because he was the handsomest.

I slowly smiled at him, lowered my eyes, and glanced away.

"Lola," he mouthed when I looked at him again. The silent volatility of the word. The way he stretched out the name matched the snarl in his eyes. That face—beautiful one moment and the next: rigid eyes, blazing nostrils, coiled lip. I'd seen that visage before, when he'd grabbed my arm at school, turning my skin red under his fingers.

I flipped my hands up in front of my chest, palms facing the sky. I shook my head. Even my mother can't restrain Lola.

I closed my eyes tightly and imagined my quinceañera: Ricardo holding me in his arms, our bodies touching. He was the one dancing my confirmation dance with me instead of my father. Regardless of the ceremony, it was he, not my father, who would make me a woman. And after the quinceañera, that was the day I would most look forward to.

The priest called us, and we began the rehearsal. I watched the damas go down the aisle with their partners, anxiously awaiting my turn.

♥

When my mother, small and stern, came downstairs, her perpetually stony face was red and her hands shook. Tía Lola had scratched her—a brutal, swollen slash across my mother's right cheek. Droplets of blood dried on her face. I stepped back, melted into the wall. Tía Lola had never harmed anyone, only herself.

I hovered next to our living room. It was cordoned off for adults and everything always remained the same there. The tiny doll statuettes my mother collected lined an oversized bookcase. She dusted them herself to ensure they remained pristine. The domino sets my father loved were displayed on the coffee table. And every day, regardless of what was happening in our house, my father sipped his coffee in a cherrywood rocking chair his grandfather made before starting his furniture business fifty-two years ago. I would peek in on the two of them when they were in this room; it's like they became different people in there.

"¿Qué pasó?" my father asked in an even tone that still conveyed his concern.

My mother's silent anger was screaming, but I could no longer hear Tía Lola's cries. For once, I was thankful. In the same way Tía Lola had spent seven years dreaming about Tío Carlos's return, I had spent those same years waiting for the day I became a woman.

"I can't deal with her anymore. She makes a spectacle of herself, and I'm trying to help her," my mother said.

I thought I heard a cluster of tears in her throat.

My father held her. "Ya, ya, ya," he said as he stroked her hair.

I'm always amazed to see her softness under his touch, all that magic contained in his hands.

"My father would die all over again to see this, a world where men leave women and never come back. Nobody says anything about Carlos. If not for him, none of this would have happened. Then everyone just stands around and laughs at her. But where is the reproach for him? He's the one who left her and she suffers for it all. She would never have done this before Carlos."

"Good thing you have me," he said, kissing her on the shoulder. "Don't worry. It's nothing. She's done this before."

They are different people together. Ones I don't know or have access to. Layers you would never see otherwise.

"Yes, but not this bad and not for so long. And I'm the one who has to answer for her. I'm the one who has to endure the whispers about her," she said and squelched any traces of fury in her voice. She turned to me, impatience growing on her face. "Stop talking to her. Stay away from Lola until after the quinceañera. No communication. None."

I stood small in front of her. "Yes, Mami." As always, her wishes would be respected.

♥

Unabashed, I blasted simmering looks at Ricardo and Estefania. I raised the peanut butter sandwich the Americans brought to our school menu to my mouth, but that's where it stayed. The smell choked me. The sun, it boiled our wooden table.

It's all I could hear—the clinking of their laughter. Rita kept her hand on my arm and said silly, mean things about Estefania. Called her Este*fea*nia. Said she's like the Americanas we see in movies, the easy Marilyns. Girls who unfastened their legs for boys without a thought to futures, to reputations, to family names.

Ricardo doesn't break eye contact with me as he flips Este*fea*nia's hair, as he leans to whisper some amusement into her ear.

This is a game we've played.

The unwritten rules of the courtship entailed breaking the rules of propriety and meeting in secret for a few minutes after school before I rushed home. And Ricardo, he would push me up against the school walls. I only let him kiss me, though. He would whisper that I was loca like my aunt. And when he talked to other girls, I cornered him in the same hallways where he whispered his desire for me. I would beat on his chest and fold into a handkerchief of grief.

♥

When Lola met Carlos at her quinceañera, it was because she had disobeyed the rules, not followed them. Her partner, a boy her father had chosen, a boy from a good family, one who would never have to leave the island and go work in the United States—that was who her father chose. Carlos was merely an attendee, not even one of the caballeros. What her parents wished for at her quinceañera was not what Lola wanted. She didn't know who or what she longed for until she met Carlos, and even though he was poor, there was something about him that could be redone, refashioned. He could easily be made into the man Lola wanted. And it was that moment that barricaded her future.

A constant picture of that stolen dance of theirs when she touched his face playfully in front of everyone. That was the way she saw her love, in snippets, highlights of the best moments. How they eclipsed the rules and the townspeople. Even though a lot could have happened in seven years, she remained turning back to those moments. Because who could have supposed the happiness, the freedom, felt on that day could lead to this?

♥

I came home and found them in the living room. Doña Olga turned to look at me, and the highlights of my life washed away from the shore. She was as formidable as my mother, two bulls in one ring. My mother's pale skin was matched by Doña Olga's dark skin. My mother's thinness to Doña Olga's thickness. Each was equal.

All the times I had watched Tía Lola cry, I had never seen how it permeated the community, how others were affected by it. I had seen the laughter, but that was just an amusement for the townspeople. Nobody had really cared.

Now, Doña Olga was here because she cared very much.

I wanted to cry, but I knew I mustn't in front of Doña Olga. But as I walked into the room to give her my regards, my mother broke out into a little smile, and Doña Olga even gave a short laugh. I looked at my mother and was grateful that she had steadied Doña Olga.

As soon as she saw Doña Olga had safely made it back to her home, my mother ran upstairs. She instantly became fierce, yelling and screaming at Tía Lola. My mother projected the future; Tía Lola negated it.

"Doña Olga just left. She said that if you don't stop, the courtship between Noelia and Ricardo will end. And if he decides after the quinceañera that he doesn't want to marry her, then who will want to come near her with an insane aunt in the same house? Everyone will think this craziness runs in the family."

"No, no, no . . ." Tía Lola repeated, and I imagined her dissolving into her bedroom floor.

♥

Tía,

I know you feel terrible, but not only has Doña Olga come over but also Ricardo has been aloof with me. This should be one of the happiest times in my life, and it's marred. Please, Tía, I urge you to think about the joy you felt during your quinceañera. Surely it was one of the most spectacular times in your life. And listening all those years to those stories about Tío Carlos, well, I couldn't wait until it was my turn. But my time has come and there has been so much angst around your grief. I say this respectfully, Tía. Just as you enjoyed your quinceañera, I wish to have

the same happy memories you did. I have always
listened to you and championed your love. I wish you
to do the same. This is not how I want to remember
my quinceañera.

Noelia

All week I had watched my mother fight with Tía Lola, forbid her to go outside and wail, and each morning, she was out there nonetheless. Tía Lola was the only person my mother could not control.

I quietly slid the letter under her door. Even though Tía Lola was nine years older than me, I had always been closer to her; she had wiped my tears when my mother was the cause of them; she plaited my hair and fashioned it the same as she always had, two French braids down her back. "When he comes back, you can even have your own room in our house," she would say to me before kissing me on the cheek.

For a moment, I envisioned myself just walking into her room, lying on her bed, and admitting my weaknesses to her. And that image gratified me for a moment, especially in thinking I could relieve her suffering, if only briefly—that that was something I had the power to alleviate. I stepped toward her door, putting my hand on it, wondering, hoping she could hear my breathing outside.

But then I heard a muffled sound—like one of her sobs in the morning. The tightness in my chest inflamed once again. I imitated my mother's stern face and stance before stomping away.

♥

Knowing she couldn't see me, I fiercely stared at her. But she lay on her back in the grass, eyes in the direction of the sky, wailing, wailing.

"Tía!" I snapped.

"Loca," I heard almost at the same time. One of the townsmen, Paolo, was snickering at our gate. He said it again, louder.

In *El qué dirán*, Santa Dávila's love was strong because it could cross borders, it could hold on. There, the community members respected her. They kept vigil with her. Not like here, where they make fun.

The front door shrieked open, and Paolo quickly moved on as my father stepped outside. Dressed for work, my father stood there for a few minutes with a cup of coffee in his hands. He too looked at the sky, but it was clear that he and Tía Lola weren't seeing the same thing. He was enjoying the sunshine, the morning, as if he couldn't hear her, see her.

When he went back inside, my mother came out and stood over her sister.

"Get up," she said to her as if she were talking to me.

Tía Lola paid her no heed and kept on. She did not notice my mother, the townsman at the gate, me, or my father.

But I saw her. Her sullied nightgown, the wet grass, the stillness of her body, except for hands clutching and clawing at her throat. In spite of all this, the sun sheathed her with its brightness. She was growing plumper. And glowed.

Stripped for so many years, Tía Lola's gathering of memories was feeding her.

♥

When I got home from school later in the day, I found a note from Tía Lola. She wrote that she wanted me to come to her room as soon as possible, that it was urgent she speak to me. I took the note and splayed it open in front of my mother. "Make her stop, please." I was shaking. "Why can't we send her to cousin Anna's house?"

When Tía Lola married Tío Carlos, her father was outraged, sputtered at her, pulled her by her hair, beat her even. This was all deeply cruel for Tía Lola, but at the end of it she had Carlos and that remedied much. But she blamed her father for Tío Carlos leaving. Her father refused to support her, and when he died a year later, she found he had followed through on his promise to cut her out of his will. And he left all of his money to my mother. Now Tía Lola was a woman without her own house, without a husband, and without a fortune.

My mother was older, and while she took care of Tía Lola, there was no familial ease between them. Tía Lola sat at our table every day knowing that all she had in the world was because my mother thought the rumors would be far worse if she were uncontained, loose in the streets. They once were close, so Tía Lola told me, but when her father turned his back on her, so did my mother. And there I stood, with the people who had been the most vicious toward Tía Lola.

♥

The clanging of the cowbells. I jumped out of bed to look out my window, and Tía Lola was not there. Jubilant, I rushed out of my room, and for the first time in weeks, there was no anger or distress lingering in the air.

My mother, sitting at the kitchen table, relaxed and smiling, said, "One more week."

Stepping onto the grass, I squinted up at the sky trying to see what Tía Lola had seen. I watched the cows lumbering in the distance before I sat down. I could smell the mango and coconut trees, the morning air. I lay on the warm ground where Lola should have been and involuntarily moaned as I felt the sun on my face, the blades of grass under me. The heat of the sun, the morning rising to possibilities, the noise and the silence. This moment, this space, was a place to dream.

All this life around me. I wondered if her wailing tuned it out. Or if Tía Lola saw it and that's why she came out here—to be born again.

♥

Her need for him made me wait for him too. I also lit candles wanting Tío Carlos to come back. I knew all their anniversaries: when he first kissed her, when he bought her the string of pearls that still chokes her neck, the number of days from the last day that he wrote. I gazed at his picture almost as much as Tía Lola did. She always described him as the most beautiful man in Puerto Rico, said he was a descendant of Arasibo, the Taíno cacique our town was named after. She said she could imagine him on the beach before *they* came and we became a different people. He was fair-skinned, though, with dark curls, not at all the man Tía Lola imagines him to be. I didn't see him on the beach, a descendant of Arasibo, but as the one who was coming to claim this land as his own.

Nonetheless, he was a man to me. I believed in him as she did, and I fulfilled his promises to her. I envisioned for her what their life could have been—should have been if he were still here or came back. I constructed the house they would live in, one like ours, spacious, white, and clean. I could hear their laughter as Tío Carlos chased Tía Lola around the house, and these were the moments when her heart could just stop because she loved him so much, and she was so delighted he was here and hers. These were the moments when she would shut her house to visitors in the daytime, would close all the doors—lock them even—pull down the window shutters, and lie next to him in bed, hold his hand under the pale-ivory silk sheet, and she would wish for a hurricane to come right at that moment and blow them away or submerge them in the tropical waters of Puerto Rico, because then the last thing she would ever know was this bliss. This everlasting happiness with Tío Carlos.

♥

She shook me awake and I suppressed a yelp. Her brown hair was no longer pinned but fell messily along her shoulders, and she wore a thin white nightgown. I thought she was coming back tomorrow. The last week of silence had been so luxurious that I thought I would cry only hearing the cowbells every morning. In the semidarkness of the night, only half of Tía Lola's body was visible, so she looked like a mere girl.

Then I remembered how she scratched my mother's face. I pulled my sheet up to my hammering heart. "Please don't be mad. Mamí forbade me to come and see you before the quinceañera. She didn't want to upset you more than you already were."

She continued to stare at me with her intense brown eyes and paused before responding. And in those few seconds, I thought about everything she had ever done for me. How she had always been there to comfort me, and how she, more so than anyone else, had made me feel loved all my life.

She reached for my hand and said softly, "You're young, Noelia. I know you must do what your mother tells you." She got up and stood by my mirror, in front of my dress. "Tell me what you think is to come. What do you hope for?" she asked in a small, sweet voice. The voice she had when Carlos first left.

She held my white quince dress in front of her. We both looked at her preening in the mirror and laughed. This Tía Lola was neither in pain, nor in anguish for love. I shushed us—these were the kind of noises I would later learn my mother envied about us. The sounds of delight that would be muffled in any other room. It's the other sound I would associate with Tía Lola: laughter that tingles and sprouts vast smiles, overtaking a room. It says there is wonder, and so much ahead, so much to come.

She pressed her body against my dress and had me hold up her hair.

"We should be engaged by next year," I said, instantly lighting up. I felt like all the times I had been in her room and she told me about Tío Carlos. I had been waiting for this day: To offer her a story of my own. And because I would be a woman hours from now, I could offer something real, not just a schoolgirl's fantasies.

I leaned forward, telling her my innermost dreams and secrets. Probably the same ones as she or maybe Tío Carlos had. Ricardo and I kissing while watching novelas. Me always getting up and meeting him at the door. I see his smile. Picture our kids, a boy and a girl, singing around the house. I always imagine myself looking at him with this simple wonder.

Lola nodded her head. I saw the sadness, the wail, come back to her eyes. "I thought that too," she said softly.

I turned away from her and checked the hour. It was time for her to leave. I had spent so many hours dreaming about Ricardo's and my future together. My body tingled at the prospect that I would be new the next day. And I wondered what it would be like to be born a woman. Would I see changes in my face? In my body? Would I be recognizable in the streets?

♥

The damas gathered around me at the church. They asked if I had seen Ricardo. That he looked handsome. They swirled around me in their pink dresses and told me I was beautiful in my white one. When it was time for the ceremony to begin, I glanced around. Tía Lola had not arrived. Upon waking that morning, I wondered if her coming to my room last night had been a dream.

The damas lined up with the caballeros, and they proceeded down the aisle in line. I watched all of them, and it was like each couple was one second in a minute, and each of their steps brought me closer to my future. Then it was my turn. My father in his fine black suit linked arms with me on my right side and my mother was on my left. She wore a purple satin dress that brought sunshine to her face. Her bare arm felt warm against mine. In slow, even paces, we walked down the aisle together. I looked straight ahead to make sure the expression on my face remained modest, though I was smiling brightly inside.

We stood to the right of the priest and he said, "Congregation, today, it is with great honor that I conduct this quinceañera mass. Noelia Nuñez and her family have long been faithful members of this church. It is with the sincerest of pleasures that I preside over this mass to usher Noelia into the rites of womanhood." He then paused, and my parents presented me with the typical quinceañera gifts. They both smiled triumphantly. My father stepped behind me and placed a gold necklace around my neck. The necklace symbolized my faith in God, myself, and the world, and in my head I added that the necklace also symbolized my faith in love, in what it meant to be a woman, and in marriage. My mother set in my hands the red rose I would place in the bouquet beneath the altar of the Virgin Mary. After I added my flower, my mother then presented me with my own new bible and a pink rosary. The three of us then participated in the Eucharist. This was just the beginning of the many rites of the day. Dancing with my father would be the last thing I did as a girl. Dancing with Ricardo would be the first thing I did as a woman.

I made my entrance into the reception hall on Ricardo's arm and was able to count how many people were actually there. Aunts, uncles, cousins, people who knew me when I was first born and others whom I had not seen since had traveled to be with me on my special day. I beamed at Ricardo. All the difficulties of the past weeks had boiled down to this, and it was how I had always envisioned it. I caught a glimpse of how Tía Lola must have felt—to be perpetually frozen in a beautiful moment. And for once, I clearly understood how difficult it could be to let go of such memories. It was a day I could easily lament the loss of and could easily play over and over again in my head.

Ricardo led me to the middle of the reception hall, to my special woven chair, with a back that fanned out around and above me. The hall was filled with balloons and flowers, and on the wall across from my chair was a sign that said "Happy Birthday, Noelia." The music stopped, and that was the cue for my father and the commencement of the next rite. My mother came toward me. She carried a white satin pillow with my high heels on top of it. My father knelt in front of me and raised my skirt (only a proper amount). He took off my flat shoes one at a time, replacing them with the heels. Everybody clapped and he took my hand to dance. My father placed his hand on my waist, and I placed mine on his shoulder. As we started to move, I saw Ricardo standing in the sidelines, waiting to dance with me next. Even though I could not wait for my dance with Ricardo, this moment slowed for me because I knew this was the last thing I would do as a girl in this world. And I took it all in, every second. Every aspect of my body was in tune with this moment. Every part of me smiled as I counted down the time. My father twirled me around the room, and in the last spin of our dance, Tía Lola strode in.

I stared at her for interminable seconds.

It was a simple ivory silk dress. The very dress she wore on her wedding day. Though tighter today, constricting.

Her hair was the same. One braid, wrapped into a bun on the left side of her head.

Everything down to the shine on her shoes was the same.

The merriment was silenced.

Everyone stared. My mother was immobilized. No one laughed like they normally did in Tía Lola's presence.

Tía Lola sauntered across the dance floor, and the tapping of her heels roared in my head.

She came over and easily pulled my father toward her, taking my confirmation dance away.

I faced my father.

My father, not sure if he should play along, moved for a beat or two with her. Then he looked at me in my white dress and finally let his arms drop, and stepped away from Tía Lola. I spun around the room to all the faces that had come to be with me. Everyone caught in that moment. How they just stood there. They all blurred, and it was not my tears. Two faces easily came into focus, Doña Olga and Ricardo. She desperately whispered in his ear, and he effortlessly nodded his head.

I wanted to reach for Ricardo, but he was already swimming away from me.

♥

Lola knew it was different this time—the wailing. It came from some other place. No longer that yearning for Carlos. For the past several weeks, since she had been mourning outside, she had returned to her room afterward, scarcely eaten anything, and barely spoken to anyone, and she unraveled the letters, one by one. And there were many. More than one would expect for a woman who had surely been abandoned. And in each one she had tried to recapture that beautiful pain in her heart that had defined her as a woman in love, given her a place in this town's history as a woman who had been left behind. She knew she would go down in stories, and there was nothing more fascinating to her than to be a woman not forgotten.

She studied those letters to resurrect her heart. What beautiful words he wrote.

She traced his words and remembered the loops of his *l*'s and the caresses of his *e*'s, but the words now lay flat on the page. She couldn't conjure anything; whatever he said began and ended on those pages. All of her senses were dead. There was no longer anything in those letters that could jump-start her heart. No more sweet fantasies during her afternoons on the veranda. Perhaps that was the greatest tragedy of all. The end of the dream seemed much more intolerable than the past seven years. Her love for Carlos, her yearning: gone. Now she would have no one, or nothing, to love.

♥

I unfurled long, cruel, deeply held screams at my mother, "You promised everything would be okay if I just stayed away from Lola. You promised. You did nothing. Nothing. You just stood there!" I felt like a statue cracking, rattled by an earthquake.

My mother, at first taken aback, stood up straight and slapped me across the face. "Young ladies do not speak to their mothers like that."

I didn't stop. Nothing could have stopped me. "That's always your response," I yelled at her. "You lied to me!"

"You think this is my fault? *Mine?* I did everything I could to make sure your quinceañera would be perfect. No, no, Noelia—I told you all your life, all your life how to behave. But it was only this year, the most important year of your life, that you decided to pay attention. This is your fault; you were always after your aunt. Let me tell you, as I have always been the one to steer you onto the right path, that it was your aunt, your beloved Tía Lola that you should be having this conversation with. She is the one who has taken your dream and crumpled it. She is the one, not me. I have always been here to support your dreams. *Me.* Not her. And you have the audacity to stand here and berate me. Sinvergüenza."

♥

"Why did you do it? How could you?" I screeched.

Tía Lola sat at her vanity and did not turn around. "I didn't want you to be a woman. It is a terrible thing to be a woman. One day, you will thank me."

I threw one of my high heels at her head. I missed, and the vanity mirror cracked and crumbled.

But Lola remained unfazed; she did not flinch or turn to look at me. "Trust me, Noelia, trust me."

♥

Nights after Lola stole my dance, I went out by the cows, waiting for Ricardo, and when he arrived, he kissed me and undressed quickly. I watched Lola fling what looked like confetti from her open window. The white paper illuminated against the blue-black sky. I pushed his shoulders up, so I could look at him one last time. Then he entered me. And I wondered what her room felt like now, devoid of its past. Had it sunk? Or risen again?

I felt shipwrecked. I imagined myself as the one landing on the untouched beaches of Puerto Rico. There is Arasibo.

He welcomes me, not knowing what I will bring.

HOLYOKE, MASS.: AN ETHNOGRAPHY

What promise she had. Incorporated in 1850, she was awarded medals and monikers: the birthplace of volleyball, "Queen of Industrial Cities," one year she was the "Paper City of the World." *Of the world.*
Paper was like gold here. The mills opening in 1849 started everything. Twenty-five paper mills at its zenith. The people boomed from 4,600 to 60,000 inhabitants from 1885 to 1920.
The streets teemed with Irish and Polish immigrants and with refined people who were able to make this small western-Massachusetts town a city where Broadway shows were previewed. A place that was about to come into its own in the shadow of New York City, but without any of the city tribulations.
That was then.
Today, there are new monikers, new people: "Highest teenage pregnancy rate in Massachusetts," "crime rate above the national average," "highest concentration of Puerto Ricans anywhere in the world outside of Puerto Rico," and girls like Veronica.

♥

What I notice most about her is her ripe body. The way her tits stick out and everything curves down the back of her skirt. She wears black sandals from Wild Pair that expose her orange-painted toenails. Gold rings populate three of the fingers on her right hand, her punching hand, and two on her left. Her lips are maroon colored, the prerequisite for any Holyoke girl. Her hair is dyed lighter than nature had ever intended and the texture has evolved. And if I sat behind her and traced the history of her hair, I would get her life story; it has gotten harsher and coarser over time. Believing it is happier at each stage.

I observed her first in the book *The Boys and Girls of Holyoke*. There were girls and boys who said they wanted to be doctors, nurses, lawyers: all the careers you see on TV. Sometimes I think Holyoke people are a cliché. Nobody will burst out dramatically here.

And who was this idealistic ethnographer anyway? Writing on a place he knew nothing about. Maybe he was from Vermont or New Hampshire, from a place that was supposed to be quaint like Massachusetts and actually was. He wasn't from around here, though; hadn't spent his life in Holyoke. But I thought it interesting that some outsider would write a whole book about us. That somebody thought us worthy enough to say over and over again, "They have hope." He came for a few days to shoot pictures and took those few precious moments caught between his eyes and the camera lens as proof of his hypothesis. But his photos, notes, observations, would be all that he was able to unearth about Holyoke, Massachusetts. Not like me, I know the ins and outs of these streets, of these people. My ethnography is the truth.

And I remember her in that book, her smile, subtle, closed mouth, and her unadornment, showing that life hadn't gotten to her yet. Perhaps she even shared the dreams of those other kids. Perhaps. She still has the same smile today, but now it shows a sexiness. Sexy at fifteen.

♥

Whenever Miss O'Donnell calls on Veronica, all she can think of when she opens her mouth is: tramp, whore, floozy. While Veronica is no more susceptible to becoming pregnant than the other girls in her class, Miss O'Donnell sees how everyone desires Veronica's beauty. And it is not her prettiness that Miss O'Donnell detests, but rather the admiring, the whispering, the rustling, and the shifting done whenever Veronica is in anyone's presence. But Miss O'Donnell knows something they don't: while Veronica is hot shit here, she wouldn't even register in someone else's world. Nowhere else would girls compare themselves to Veronica to see how their jeans matched up, their shoes, their lipstick color, their right shade of hair. Only here, especially in Miss O'Donnell's class.

But lucky for Miss O'Donnell, she doesn't have to call on Veronica too often. Veronica is one of those girls who doesn't talk much in class. Since kindergarten, Veronica has rarely raised her hand, and this pattern of barely doing anything has followed her into her high school years and will inevitably follow her for the rest of her life. She usually sits there with a hard expression on her face, popping her gum. Any ounce of intelligence she may have had at birth will surely never surface and rescue her from this life.

For a bit of amusement, Miss O'Donnell chooses

Veronica today. When Veronica is called on in class, butterflies gnaw at her stomach, and it's sometimes worse than being with boys. Veronica wants to ignore Miss O'Donnell, but she is one of those teachers who will call you out. Mad before class even starts. So Veronica speaks inaudibly, but then not being able to discern Miss O'Donnell's facial expression, she speaks louder, rushing forward with her words.

What Veronica doesn't know is that Miss O'Donnell is really just mulling over how she will unwind in front of the TV tonight. As soon as she gets home, she will forget about this day, this week, and will undoubtedly calculate how many days to retirement, even though she knows the number is 635, but each day she likes to count again. Sometimes she doesn't include the weekends or holidays when she needs a bit more to hold on to. She will dream about her life after all of this and assure herself that it will not be too late to be happy. She will flip through cruise and vacation brochures (she makes sure to receive new ones each month) and imagine herself in an exotic place. She sees Puerto Rico on the list of destinations, and while she wants to stay far away from anything Puerto Rican, it looks so pretty in brochures: beautiful beaches, pink and yellow houses, grand hotels, and plenty of white people. And she can't fathom these Holyoke Puerto Ricans with that place. But maybe the Puerto Ricans there are different, more couth. When Miss O'Donnell goes to sleep that night, she will dream of herself with another retired teacher, pink and plump just like her, turning red in the hot Puerto Rican sun. They will laugh at the people who work at their beach resort as they rub suntan lotion on each other and discuss how yes, they are different, so much more polite and unnoticeable than the Puerto Ricans in Holyoke. And there, she will not see anyone like Veronica. Finally, in the streets, Miss O'Donnell will be the one looked at.

When Veronica notices the dismissive expression in Miss O'Donnell's green eyes, her words, like always, trail off to the inaudible. But no matter, her classmates are certainly not concerned with Miss O'Donnell and what she considers important. What they want to know is who Veronica is fucking and if it's true that she once gave Ralfy a blow job at the Holyoke Mall.

Maria slips Veronica the question book that has been passed around the classroom since Miss O'Donnell took roll thirty-five minutes ago. There is a question on every page and everybody has chosen a number as an alias. Page three asks, Who will get pregnant next: Veronica Diaz, Tiffany Suarez, or Elizabeth Gomez? Veronica stares down at number four, number nine, and all the other numbers on the page who have one simple answer to that question: VD. Veronica scans the room and realizes that her classmates are watching to see her reaction.

She reviews the question again, all the VDs, and the one "Ralfy fucks her all the time. She has to be pregnant." Veronica covers her mouth with her fist, she doesn't know why she's the one they always talk shit about. Then she writes *TS*—she already has a baby anyway—and passes the book.

What differentiates Veronica from most of the other Holyoke girls is that she's an in-between girl. Never is she unaware of the role she has to play, she never leaves home without her hardness, she practices how to fight when she is alone, and constantly scrolls through all the other things she has to do in order to avoid even more fights. But she has this squishy little heart inside that sometimes presses on her so hard that she has to cry. Never in front of her girls because she knows that even though she has been friends with them for many years, that could change at any moment. But she lets it all out in front of Ralfy, because it's okay to cry in front of your boyfriend, because that is what girls are supposed to do, even Holyoke girls. So now she presses her nails into her palm to distract herself because breaking down in front of her classmates would mean total dissolution, and no one, not even Cassandra, Veronica's best friend and the most popular girl at school, could help her out. Veronica takes a moment and visualizes something she truly hates. Firms her heart up. Glances back at Maria and rolls her eyes, so everyone can see, can see that she doesn't give a fuck.

While Veronica is not the most popular girl at Holyoke High, she is certainly one of the prettiest, and her uncontested friendship with Cassandra ensures that very few girls will step to her. Veronica has gotten into a few fights but not since she started high school. However, if she were in the ranks of the untouchable girls, like Cassandra, people would never talk about her. The rumors about her wouldn't have that *slightly* nasty tone, but she is popular enough that they are certainly not all-out malicious.

"I like how everyone thinks I'm gonna get pregnant," Veronica declares. Although still bothered from class, she knows she has to mention it, otherwise she will come off like a punk. She has to make sure to laugh loud at lunch, talk big, or do something that will get her noticed so no one will think she's been affected in the least.

"Even if you were, what's the big deal? They could have said a lot nastier shit," Maria replies.

There isn't a time when Veronica does not remember being friends with Maria. Going into high school, they haven't been as close, but Veronica realizes that it would be worse to end things with Maria than to just go along with their friendship. There would be too much drama if she stopped talking to her. Maria is average looking, but has a great sense of style and, most importantly, she's tough. People are less apt to fuck with Maria. She has a big mouth, and everyone knows she's willing to get down if necessary. In short, Maria is cool. A person like Maria is what a girl like Veronica needs.

"Anyway, have you seen Ralfy yet?" Cassandra interjects.

"No, I haven't seen him in like a week and he's never on Chestnut Street when I'm looking for him. He's been acting shady lately. I think he's playing me. But I don't know with who because everybody knows I go out with him."

"Yeah, well, you never know about these chicken-heads. Maybe he's been arrested," Cassandra offers.

"Maybe, but I figured that he would've called or someone else would've told me. I don't know . . . this shit is so wack."

"Are you gonna break up with him?" Maria asks.

"No, not yet. I wanna find out what the deal is first."

The white girl from their class, Gail, the one who

lives in the Flats—a Puerto Rican section of Holyoke, even though, if truth be told, most of Holyoke is Puerto Rican even if white people have their own neighborhoods and outnumber them—walks by the three girls and says, "Hi."

Maria leans in. "What about her? I heard she's been talking to Ralfy."

Veronica dwells on that hi, and she sees Gail stop to talk to Frankie, the only Puerto Rican boy at this school who Veronica, Maria, and Cassandra would even entertain going out with. Veronica sees the way Gail giggles and flips her dirty brown hair. She refuses to really believe this girl could be competition. But Veronica ruptures.

"Gail, come here."

"Hey," Gail says, not sure what's going on.

"I hear you're real tight with my man. Is that true?"

Others turn to look at them in the cafeteria and Maria laughs.

"I know him in passing, but that's about it," Gail says shaking her head and taking a step back.

"Well make sure to keep it that way." Veronica stares Gail down until she knows she has given her classmates something new to talk about. Normally, bringing fear into a white girl's eyes is not what makes Veronica feel strong. White people don't know how to fight. In fact, fights with white girls won't even make a reputation. Only fights with other Puerto Rican girls and the few black girls who live here count. But today, she needs this. Veronica turns back to Maria and Cassandra and says, "She's lucky she doesn't get smacked. If I catch her talking to him, it's on."

♥

The Irish. What rabble-rousers. Being the first wave of immigrants made them puff up with power. They proliferated in the mill industry. And knowing they were the dominant majority, they started demanding more, more, and more. Setting off the labor unions. But all that was short-lived. The mills then purposely started recruiting French Canadians—considered to be more docile. The Irish couldn't be rooted out though, and vestiges of the Irish still remain. To this day, everyone in Holyoke still attends the Saint Patrick's Day parade. Can you imagine anything more absurd than a bunch of Puerto Ricans at a Saint Patty's Day parade?

♥

In South Holyoke, the Flats, Up the Hill, and on Chestnut Street, the Puerto Rican girls walk in silence, hoping for invisibility if they are alone or in pairs, but more than two and they feel safe, like they can beat anyone down, like they own the streets. Trekking home with Cassandra after school, Veronica's heart beats erratically when she spies a group of Puerto Rican girls occupying the stoop ahead of them. This is when she and Cassandra are wary of their volume; they lower their voices and try not to rouse anyone's attention. Cassandra's reputation only extends so far. They're no longer at Holyoke High, and they don't know these girls. It's always this way with them. Every day, the heart pounding. The only time they can be carelessly loud, throw their shoulders back, and be noticed is around white people.

Veronica and Cassandra make it to the girls, and Veronica listens real hard to make sure that nothing is said under their breaths. While Veronica would hate to fight, she knows she must if anything was said to her or about her, especially in front of someone else. Cassandra keeps chatting; her silence would draw more attention to her, but she also knows enough to not be too loud. She's telling Veronica about a party next week. Veronica pays attention to Cassandra, but she strains her ears to hear the other girls. Then she very softly hears, "Corny bitches." Veronica's heart sprints, and she slows her pace. She is about to turn around and glare at the four girls, but she glances at Cassandra and, to her relief, she hasn't heard anything. She just keeps talking and Veronica knows she's saved this time. She wills herself to believe that she may have misheard or that nothing was uttered at all. But Veronica's thrashing heart doesn't subside for another few blocks. Sometimes she wonders what it is like to be white and not have to deal with this shit every day of her life.

When Veronica gets home, she lies on her bed, listening to the cars in the alley, the noise of the TV in the living room, and the raised voices of her mother and her mother's boyfriend Willie. They aren't necessarily fighting, they always talk real loud to each other. She rolls her eyes, turns on her side, and dwells on Ralfy because that's all she has to think about. She wonders where he could be, and why she hasn't heard from him. Veronica doesn't like being home, but appreciates that there are always a few minutes of refuge there, where she can let her mind wander. But inevitably, she is pulled toward fighting with her mother, Willie, or her little sister Gigi.

Veronica can hear her sister bossing around some

other girl in the alleyway, and she wants to go out there and tell Gigi she's being out of pocket. But instead, Veronica puts a pillow over her eyes and hopes she falls asleep before she hears the girl start to cry.

♥

"But Maria said she saw him last night at Tito's house. Do you want to see if he's on Chestnut now?" Cassandra says.

"Is that what she told you? She didn't even mention that to me. What the fuck is going on?" Veronica says.

They walk through Jackson Parkway, and for the first time in weeks, Veronica spots Ralfy on the playground across the street. Her disappointment that he is there and hasn't called is deflating. "You think I should be a bitch, or act nice?" she asks Cassandra.

Cassandra shrugs. "Let's see what he has to say."

She looks down at the cracked sidewalk and tries to let the happiness at seeing him overrun her. "Ralfy," she calls from across the street.

He acknowledges her with a nod and heads toward her.

"So what's up? I haven't seen you," Veronica says as she leans over to kiss him.

"Nothing, you know, same old shit. Cops were sweating me, so I've been chilling at my mom's house in Springfield and I just got back last night."

"Nice to let me know. I've been looking for you. I beeped you like ten times."

"Oh, my batteries died, and I didn't get new ones until this morning."

"Really?"

"Yeah, I'm serious," he says as he encircles her waist with his arm and pushes her forward so she leans against his body. "Next time I'll make sure to call you. Come on, don't be mad. I haven't seen you in a while; I don't want to fight. Defend me here, Cassandra. Tell her to chill."

Veronica looks at Ralfy's bronze face and sees that beautiful grin, that smile she really wants to believe exists only for her. It breaks the hardness of his face, and he seems like two boyfriends at once. Since she was thirteen, she's seen him at all the parties, and even then she wanted to be the girl he invited into hallways to rap to. He entwines his fingers with hers, bites his lip, and presses his forehead against hers, until Veronica has to return his wondrous smile. Despite his bullshit, Veronica is elated Cassandra is here to observe this moment, so that all those people who talk shit can know, can see, he really does love her. She pulls back and kisses him on the lips and asks him what he's up to now. He says that he's waiting for Tito, but he'll call her later so she can come over.

When Veronica and Cassandra stride away, Veronica beams with energy. She turns back to admire Ralfy and loves the way he looks with his hands in his pocket, a hoodie over his curly hair. She feels the heat of her heart spread. These are the only times she can be connected to her feelings, when she is with Ralfy, because even Holyoke girls are allowed to hope for love.

♥

Veronica squeals with delight as Ralfy tickles her and

tackles her onto his bed. She kicks her legs underneath him.

"Oh my god, let me tell you how at school I was voted most likely to get pregnant."

He slaps her stomach and kisses it. "You want a baby from me? Shit, I can give you a baby."

"Only if you want one," she says coyly. "If I had a baby I could just leave my house and have my own shit. I wouldn't have to go to school anymore, and we could be together more." She strokes his head on her stomach. "But my mom keeps giving me speeches about not getting pregnant."

Veronica's mother stopped asking her where she spends the night. It is safer to think Veronica is at Cassandra's house. It is easier for her to jump to that conclusion—the one that has the safe ending. If she had to think any harder, then her imagination would unravel like red ribbons and she may have to think about her little girl fucking and how their lives have started to follow the same trajectory. Then there would be no more choices about what little Veronica is doing—no alternatives for mother or daughter to mull over. Just knowledge of what lies ahead.

"She still thinks I'm a virgin," Veronica says and laughs. She had waited to lose her virginity until she was fifteen, even though no one believed her. They all thought there was no way. But this was one way she could be different from all the other Holyoke girls.

"Seriously, if she only knew how many times I pounded that pussy."

"Eww, don't say it like that." Veronica slaps Ralfy's arm. Sex with Ralfy isn't like in the movies, where some guy comes over to the woman's house with flowers and he's willing to do just about anything to please her. The woman is always wearing pretty matching underwear, she always seems to know what to do in bed, and they always orgasm at the same time. With Ralfy, clothes don't have to be off. They don't use protection; she doesn't think about the size of his dick or if he's making her feel good. She just thinks that sex isn't as great as she had heard it was. When he finishes, he rolls off her. And it is over just like that. She doesn't know there can be better, just that this isn't as good. And this is the whole world for her. Sometimes I wish I could reach down and put my mouth over hers, breathing into her a new life.

♥

Down in the Flats, cars filled with the Polish rammed Puerto Ricans against the red-brick apartment buildings. The *za chlebem* immigrants, once landless, who came to Holyoke to claim their own parcels and reap from the mills, once again felt the loss of green or concrete under their feet, and they decided to fight. But the smashing of the Puerto Ricans did not keep them out. They broke through. And now, the Polish don't even remain like the Irish. No vestiges to mark that the Polish were actually once here.

♥

Every Thursday, Veronica heads to Cassandra's house. It's only the two of them because they both live in South Holyoke, and Maria moved to Jarvis Heights, an apartment complex in another part of town, a few years ago. It's a nice spring night and while Veronica waits for Cassandra to come down to the stoop, she checks her beeper to make sure she hasn't missed a beep from Ralfy. She hasn't. She tries to pinpoint when this shadiness first started and can't find a clear-cut difference between before and after. Because, if truth be told, Ralfy has always acted this way. Guys are supposed to hold girls at a distance. Veronica never believed he would act in an extraordinary way, but with all her suspicions, only now is it starting to get to her.

"V, oh my god, look at what my mother found," Cassandra exclaims as she skips down the stairs and plops down next to Veronica.

"Oh shit," Veronica says when she opens the book, *The Boys and Girls of Holyoke*. "Are you in this too? There is a picture of me somewhere in here."

"Yup, look, there I am. Look at this shit. I said I wanted to be a nurse. Can you believe that shit?"

"That's so funny. You want to be a nurse for real? Let me see what I told that man," Veronica says turning the pages to find her picture. She stares at herself.

"What did you say?"

"Oh, I said I didn't know." Veronica barely recognizes herself in the picture. Doesn't believe she was ever that young. That there was a time she didn't have this body or left the house without makeup. Staring down at her quote on the page, she now remembers that day, that man and his camera, his notepad, and all of his questions. She had wanted to tell him her "career dreams," but some of her classmates were standing nearby and she didn't want to sound corny. So she told him she didn't know.

The man kept asking if she was sure. Veronica knew she disappointed him and wasn't sure if she would make it into the book. She was exhilarated when she saw herself in the group photo on the cover, and she had a page to herself on the inside. When she read everyone else's answers to the man's questions, she gasped and punched the book. Even if she had whispered it in his ear, she wished she had told him.

Cassandra pulls out a smoke and says, "Look, there's Jeanette. She just had a baby. Guess she won't be a doctor now."

"Do you think any of them meant it?"

"Probably not. That is some shit you say when you're young. I bet most of them don't remember saying any of this," Cassandra responds.

Veronica nods because, sitting on the stoop now with Cassandra by her side, the book on her lap, she feels her heart press against her. She instinctively pulls out a cigarette, hoping the smoke will reach all the way down and shroud her heart.

Cassandra turns on the boom box she brought down with the book. It's Thursday and from six to eight they listen to clubhouse dance music, softly singing the words to the songs of Judy Torres, TKA, Cynthia, Coro, and India. This is one of Veronica's most cherished pastimes. Every week without fail, Puerto Ricans all over Western Mass., in their cars or their kitchens, tune into STCC FM, and they all know the words by heart. Most of the songs are about heartbreak. Veronica's favorites are when the guy sings about how he made a mistake with a girl, how he fucked up and now wants her back. That that could actually happen.

Veronica has always imagined herself sitting with Cassandra doing this on Thursday nights, but now, flipping through the book, she wonders what the years will bring. For once, she thinks the future isn't written. This fills her with sadness, and just a small pocket of hope. The girls hawk the cars going by. When they peep guys they know, and walk over to the double-parked cars, Veronica is left knowing that if she were to ever leave Ralfy, one of these double-parked guys would love to step.

♥

The last to arrive, to work in the tobacco fields, were the Puerto Ricans. They came in the fifties. Not the fifties memorialized on TV. These people came to work. Not in offices. No clean, crisp, white shirts at the end of the day. No nice homes to return to by six o'clock. No doting wives. They came to work with their hands. Maybe just like they did in Puerto Rico. Tobacco instead of sugar cane. By the time they came, though, everything was almost gone. All the promise. All the upward spirals. All the paper like gold.

♥

Last weekend, Veronica and Cassandra had a girl's night instead of going to a party like they normally do. But Maria didn't want to be involved; she went out without them. Veronica and Cassandra were excited to do something different. Just like when they were little girls, they wore pink and blue plush pajamas with clouds and small yellow thunderbolts, watched *The Little Mermaid*, and undid each other's hair. Bangs hair-sprayed into ski slopes were finger-combed out. Bunned hair was unfurled and let loose. Their faces stripped down. Cheeks glistening from the removal of makeup. Most of the night they laughed with their mouths full of popcorn—wide and with abandon.

They had planned to do the same this weekend, but by the end of Monday afternoon, Veronica heard that Gail was grinding on Ralfy at a party and she will not be punked any longer. She turns to the right and the left in the mirror. Wearing her baggy jeans, black boots, and black halter top, she wonders if she looks pretty enough tonight because, like most girls, she thinks beauty is the best way to keep a man. And she's right: in Holyoke and at her age, that's all there is. Gail with her small tits and flat ass can't be competition, plus Ralfy always said he would never date a white girl. But Gail *is* different. She's not a regular white girl. She's gone out with Puerto Ricans, and a long time ago, in elementary school, she was friends with Maria. A month ago, Veronica never even paid attention to Gail, but now Veronica watches to see what Gail's wearing or if she's hanging around Puerto Ricans because if she is, that changes her status, makes her more competition.

The thing about Holyoke girls is that they don't realize how important other girls are to them. Their hearts pound for each other when they walk into parties. The way the night unfolds has nothing to do with rapping to a new guy, but if they fight with another girl. That is more life altering than what boy they end up with. Will the girl's friends jump in? Who won't talk to her

Monday morning? One mechanism changes and they have to wait to see how all the other parts will react. Mutation.

Between the crowded bodies at the party, Veronica sees Maria with her arms wrapped around Ralfy's neck. Across the room, she can clearly see Ralfy's trademark smile beaming at Maria. Veronica turns to Cassandra and says, "What is this shit?"

"Easy. You don't know anything for sure yet," Cassandra says.

Veronica marches over to Ralfy, purposely bumps into Maria, and pulls him outside. "You've been mad shady lately. If you're cheating on me, then just let me know because I don't want to put up with this shit. I've been hearing a lot of noise about you messing around with Gail. Is that true?"

"Veronica, baby, please. You keep saying things like that. Maybe it's you, huh? You got another man?"

"Don't turn this on me. Why were you dancing with Maria like that? Are you fucking her?"

He laughs. "Veronica, why would I mess with your girl? She's not even cute. We were just dancing," he says, flashing his smile at her.

"You're a fuckin' liar," Veronica says as she slams her fists into his chest.

I wonder if she ever sat down and thought for just one second that perhaps love doesn't exist. Because who has she ever known that has ever been in love? Not her parents, not her neighbors, and most certainly not her friends. How is it that you can begin to believe in something when you have never seen proof of it? And weren't these notions of love based on movies and books that in all other respects did not reflect her life?

But girls will be girls.

Girls think they'll be better than their mothers—burst out dramatically, have an effect on a man's life. In Holyoke, girls wanting to be in love is as inevitable as fighting in the streets.

Veronica hauls back into the party. "Are you fucking my man?" she huffs in Maria's face.

Veronica doesn't bother to wait for Maria to part her maroon-colored lips. Her heart knows the answer. Veronica does what she must and smacks Maria's head back into the wall. Before Maria can remember who she is, Veronica grabs her by the hair and smashes her head against her knee. The party people roar and cheer Veronica on. She knocks Maria to the ground and stops only when Ralfy pulls her off. When he envelops her, Veronica's heart bursts.

And she does the unthinkable.

Veronica starts to cry.

THE SIMPLE TRUTH

Mr. Jack Agüeros provides a very idealized portrayal of Julia de Burgos in his introduction to *Song of the Simple Truth*, what he proclaims is a volume of her complete works. But as one reads his introduction, one finds that some of her poems are irrevocably lost. His version of her love affair with Dr. Juan Isidro Jimenes Grullón is very different from any of the others I've read. Agüeros is the only one who depicts her as a heartbreaker; other portrayals hint she suffered some abuse. Some say she was a dipsomaniac because she could not have Dr. Grullón, and that she ultimately died on the streets of Spanish Harlem, on 104th and Fifth Avenue, like a common pauper because this great man took his love away. Even the ex-president of the Dominican Republic, Mr. Juan Bosch himself, believes that.

But I dislike that story. It makes her seem frivolous— like any other woman I could pass on the street. So I accept Mr. Jack Agüeros's word on it. I suspect he wants to see Julia in the same light I do.

I am careful where I step in my apartment. The first thing I will do tomorrow, well maybe Sunday, is clean this place or else I will end up with Fluffy's hair on all my clothes. I lock him out of my room to keep my dress free of his hair. I spent at least four weeks looking for this dress. It's black, knee-length, with red lace flowers. When I saw it, I imagined Julia in it looking like a coquette. I carefully model my hair after the photo of her that Jack Agüeros chose for his cover, the one where she is looking straight at you and smiling as if she shares secrets with the person taking the picture. I throw a red scarf over my shoulders and have to laugh. Everybody dressed up tonight as if it were the 1940s. I take one last look in the mirror and hope I will be as striking as Julia.

♥

Stepping into the empty ballroom, I take it all in without the throngs of partygoers set to arrive in two hours. Tonight is the third annual ball to benefit the Julia de Burgos Cultural House. I interned there last summer, and they offered me a job after I graduated from Barnard. I started in July as an assistant to the archivist, Jose, who let me head up the exhibition for the ball because he plans to retire next year. My ex-boyfriend Alex usually accompanied me to parties and tonight, without him, I feel nervous. A night where the end is a mystery.

I met Alex my first year at Barnard, and we had been together ever since. This past fall he went to Harvard for graduate school. Everyone thought he would propose to me before he left, so that we could be married by the time he finished. He did ask, but I said no. Probably the bravest thing I have ever done. My mother and father clashed on many things, but their thought processes were always parallel. Her disdain for something ran as deep as his love for the same thing, but at the end of the day, they disentangled themselves from their views and created a storied love that I have yet to find with any boyfriend.

Jose waves and gives me a kiss on the cheek. He extends his arm to me and I feel giddy. He has shared his knowledge about the Cultural House with me ever since I began working here and has been my steadfast supporter. He adores Julia as much as I do, but in a different way. He has grown to admire her over the years as a historian putting together the pieces of her life, which has often proven to be a formidable task. I worship her like a child mesmerized by the strength of her father.

We take in the room together, and as we stop in front of a picture of Julia in Cuba, Jose leans in and says, "You look lovely. Like a young Julia de Burgos. Maybe you'll meet your Grullón tonight, but with a happier ending, of course." In the photo, she is standing between two men, laughing merrily. She is wearing a white knee-length dress, and while there is another pretty woman in the picture, she is hardly noticeable. Julia has a quiet beauty, the kind that enters a room unobtrusively, not turning heads with a big fuss or a red dress, but standing in a corner and waiting patiently for your eyes to fall upon it, knowing they ultimately will.

My mother doesn't like the premise for my exhibition. The display revolves around the notion of Julia's love affairs. I spent countless hours poring over books, talking to professors, and hunting down pictures from El

Centro in order to put it together. Pictures of Julia and various rumored paramours are hung around the room, and underneath is a summary of the evidence that a particular poem had been written for that man.

When I first told her about it, her exact words were "Isn't it sad that a woman can do a great many things, is still noted today as the greatest poet in Puerto Rico, yet all we are concerned about is who she was sleeping with."

But she should have known that the exhibition was a way to honor my father.

♥

While sitting at a table with some other coworkers, Rosanna whispers in my ear, "Maceo is here."

I flutter inwardly. He looks the same as he did last summer when he interned with me. Rosanna and I would take turns giggling whenever we saw him in the office. At lunch we would have daily updates of Maceo sightings.

Maceo catches me looking at him, and I blush as he begins to make his way over.

The night that Julia met Grullón, she was at a party in the Dominican Republic. Her first time in the country, she is escorted by Dr. Juan Bosch, an intellectual and the future president, and she is his prize. It remains dubious where his love runs. But Grullón stages a coup d'état that night and every night thereafter as he is the one the majority says she loves enduringly; their names, if not their bodies, entwined forever.

When Maceo reaches us, he gives Rosanna and me a kiss on the cheek.

"This all looks amazing, Maricarmen," he says, his eyes falling on the different pictures.

"Thank you. I've loved living in Julia's world."

"Your father would be proud."

I beam. He remembered.

"So what's next?" Maceo says as he smiles to his eyes. He is the kind of person everyone has a good word about. He is the kind of man I would watch from afar.

"I just go back to the mundane everyday stuff after this."

♥

My mother arrives with her colleagues, and as always she is in the front charging the air wherever she steps. She is the woman in the red dress. Before even finding her table, she comes over.

"Let's dance, you look too pretty to be sitting down," she says to me.

She twirls me around the floor to the sounds of salsa from her time. I am clumsy and cannot keep up with her. The band then begins to play a rendition of "En Mi Viejo San Juan," and I hear the excited murmuring of the dancers in recognition of this classic. I am determined to keep up with her. The song must conjure up in them, as it does in me, memories of their youth, their parents or grandparents, whether on the Island or here. My father always played this song, always remembering his parents' home.

He came to New York in his twenties, right after he

graduated from college, and after three months of being in law school, he met a Cuban, Alfredo Montañez, who became my father's lifelong friend. Alfredo told him how there were throngs of Puerto Ricans living uptown and that he would take my father there sometime. They could go out dancing, meet women, and it would be just like being in Puerto Rico. Alfredo escorted my father around El Barrio, and he was hooked. Arriving in New York on the heels of a new radicalism, my father fell in love with all the political organizing that was going on at the time. He quickly became involved and told his father that he wanted to be a tenant lawyer. There were a lot of people who lived in the filth of the projects, and he spent the rest of his life championing the rights of the people Alfredo had shown him.

My father was the one who introduced me to the works of Julia de Burgos. When he and my mother first met, they spent countless hours reading each other Latin American poetry. "Those were the sixties," he would joke whenever he told that story. It was his turn to tell me a bedtime story every other night, and he was the best at it. He would pull all these figures from history and make them come alive. He told tales of a young Pablo Neruda and how his words would set a people free, of the Young Lords and how they had hung a Puerto Rican flag from the Statue of Liberty. A few times a month my father told me about Julia because they were both from Carolina, Puerto Rico. He wanted to imbue in me the notion that there were extraordinary people from where he came from. He told me of how Nobel Prize–winning poets singled her out. In all the world, this woman from this tiny island was writing poems that floated from island to island, country to country; a voice that easily could have been obscured, reaching all those disparate parts of the world.

♥

As Rosanna gets up to dance with one of our young interns, she winks at me, as if she is going to feast on him. I laugh and hum along to the music. He doesn't dance very well, so I watch her lead him around the dance floor.

"Men shouldn't be allowed to not know how to dance," she says when she comes back. "What a disappointment." She critiques everyone's dance skills until she sees Maceo approaching and brings up how we almost kissed last summer. I was still with Alex, so I had stopped myself. I smack her leg so she will be quiet before he gets to us. Maceo comes up behind me, leans over, and whispers in my ear if I would like to dance.

In an interview about Julia, Dr. Juan Bosch recalls an incident at a party in Cuba where Julia—he remembers her as beautiful—is going from partner to partner until her lover, the infamous heartbreaker Dr. Jimenes Grullón, shows up. He pulls her gently aside, and their loud words overshadow the festive mood. And all the good Dr. Bosch can remember after that is Julia fleeing into the night. He knew the affair had somehow been broken. He goes up to Grullón and shouts, "What happened?" Without waiting for an answer, he leaves in search of Julia, but alas does not find her. I imagine

Dr. Bosch slams his fist down on the table at this point in the interview because his affection for her was resilient. Throughout the years, he hears bits and pieces of her life, snatches of conversations that have floated over miles of land and over the Caribbean Sea, which has washed out the truth of any of it. And then he hears of her death in the streets, and Dr. Bosch weeps in ways men are never supposed to.

I smile weakly at Maceo and tell him I am too tired to dance, that my mother wore me out. The difference between Julia and me is that she just looks like the quiet beauty but inside she is the woman in the red dress, and I am not.

♥

One of my favorite pictures in the exhibit is the one where Julia's body is being returned to Puerto Rico. This photo has nothing to do with Julia's romantic life per se but is about how much the public cherished her. In his book, Jack Agüeros tells a story of standing with a friend in front of a stoop in East Harlem and a group of men come around a corner with one woman among them. They were all drunk, people that would easily be dismissed. The friend points out that the woman is Julia de Burgos. Agüeros, not knowing who she is, had just taken her for a drunkard. His friend tells him that she is the greatest living Puerto Rican poet.

She died on the streets of East Harlem and was buried in Potter's Field. Potter's Field, where the nameless, the faceless, the poor, go. When the ambulance picked her up, all the paramedics saw was a body that must not have had any identification, a woman who died on the streets of East Harlem alone, with no family, with no one by her side, a woman with the smell of alcohol on her, and they must have thought that no one in all the world could care about a woman like this. And for a while, her body remained underground with the rest of New York's forgotten.

There is a macabre rumor that Agüeros relates: that part of Julia's legs were cut off so she could fit in the small pine box the City of New York provided for her burial. But Puerto Rico loved her—it would have outfitted her with more than just a plain pine box. They would have accommodated her legs, all of her limbs.

The coffin, when it finally reached the San Juan airport, was draped with a Puerto Rican flag. In the photo, people from all over Puerto Rico stand at the airport, like they would await returning family members; even though they may have never seen her in life, they have all known her. Have held her picture, read her poems, fallen in love with something . . . enough to give up their work days, give up cooking for their families, give up taking care of their kids, all for a glimpse of a casket draped in a Puerto Rican flag. But it is more than a coffin; they know who lies in it: "La vida, la fuerza, la mujer."

I recognize their love—the way I think we should all be loved.

♥

"Well, from what I hear Maceo is quite the little star at PRLDEF. His father was a lawyer, and Maceo also plans on going to law school," Rosanna says.

"Oh, in that case, my mother will think he's perfect for me," I reply.

"Hey, well your mother's not going to be the one sleeping with him."

"Whoa, we're not quite there yet."

"Maricarmen! You're not a virgin? Are you?"

"No, I'm just extremely choosy as to who I have sex with."

"Well, how many people have you had sex with?"

"Just two."

"Two? You might as well be a virgin."

We start to laugh.

"Shut up. If and when I find the right guy, I will be glad to make it three."

"Well, I hope you're not waiting for Prince Charming, Cinderella," Rosanna says before getting up to dance with the intern again.

Since I broke up with Alex, I haven't dated anyone. Since I was young, I have always been reclusive. And with the breakup, it's like I regressed further back into myself, into the world my father created for me. And too often, I have found comfort in that.

♥

My mother and I stand shoulder to shoulder as we have for many years. We are in front of the snapshot taken outside my father's schoolhouse, and he stands two children down from Julia. I have relished this photo for years.

My mother gazes at my father in the picture. "I wish I had known him then."

He has been dead for two years. To her, it must seem easy for me. I go to work every day, and it is like he is there with me, sharing another anecdote about Latin America or Julia.

The last fight they had was almost a year before my father died. I came home to surprise them one weeknight, and walking down the hall, I could hear my mother yelling. "How would you like me to tell Maricarmen about your twenty-two-year-old? Let me guess, she writes you love poems, and you swoon like a pendejo."

I quietly retreated from the apartment. That was a week before we found out he was sick. After that it didn't matter what he had done in his life, though I am sure this is the only thing he needed to regret. He left his girlfriend, and he and my mother spent those last eight months together like they had in the sixties. But when he died, the memories of their love died too. My mother's anger over his betrayal resurfaced. She had only temporarily swallowed it, and now it was like she had forgotten they were ever in love.

She turns to me and asks why I like Julia so much. "Do you like her just because your father did?"

"Maybe at first, but not now. She's under my skin. She's my idol."

"Idols always break, Maricarmen. Have you ever heard how she was a prostitute? A woman who would be with men for what they could give her. She was very poor when she came to this country."

"Yeah, I've heard. But like anything with Julia, it is a chimera. So many stories, who knows what is really true."

My mother stares at me. "That doesn't bother you? What would make you stop loving her?"

"Not everyone has to fall off their pedestals just because they can't live up to it."

"What about the people who are disappointed? Those who put you there?"

"They should know that people sometimes have to come down, but the fact that you put them there should mean something, should ensure their permanent place on that pedestal." I pause. I know what I have to say. "Papi loved you more than anything, more than Julia, poetry, and so much more than . . . anybody else in the world."

"I think I'm the only one who can measure his love."

Emboldened, I continue, "No, I don't think so. You can't see anymore. Do you think you can ever get back to that place, to the way things were?"

"Maricarmen, some things can never be undone. Especially with memory. Once you know something like that, you always know it. You can never go back to that untainted place, even if you wanted to."

"So you don't think you could ever love him again the same way?"

"No, not ever."

"I still love him. He's my father. That never changed anything for me."

"That's because he wasn't your husband. You hadn't given him thirty years of your life."

"A different love, but love the same."

"A blind love. Not the same kind of love at all."

"Is that why you hate Julia so much?"

My mother uncomfortably talks to the picture. "It

seems silly, but yes. I think she was your father's perfect woman. Your father was never much for fanfare. He was quiet, like you. He could get lost in her poetry, and in his reveries, it seemed that he reached a sort of nirvana. Like he had met his ideal woman and they had reached their perfect place. It's hard to know that you are not necessarily what your husband wanted but instead what he had to settle for in real life."

"Mother, Father loved you. I can't imagine he settled for anyone. When he knew he only had so many days left to live, he spent them with you. He could have left and ran around the world, but he didn't."

"Maybe he just didn't want to lose you, his girl."

"He knew I would love him regardless, and I didn't live at home, so if he wanted to be a bachelor, he could have just gotten an apartment in New York and seen me anytime."

"I wish he hadn't left me with that stain. In the end, I'm left to deal with all the consequences. And some days I hate him so much, even though I don't want to because he's dead, and he did everything he could to redeem himself."

"Maybe not now, maybe in a few more years, but there is always a way back."

I look back at the picture of my father so close to Julia. With my mother standing next to me, Julia now looks different in the picture. Distracted. Smiling, but not a smile for that place, that moment. And I wonder if that is how my mother sees her. My mother remains silent, and I think back to how she was not very good at storytelling—she would tell me fairy tales, but would always lapse into some feminist manifesto, completely changing the story. The first time one of my teachers asked the class if we knew the story of Cinderella, I raised my hand and repeated what my mother had told me. My teacher looked at me puzzled and burst out laughing. She was what my mother would have called a slave to the patriarchy. Nonetheless, I never again offered my mother's version of a story.

♥

The event will be over in an hour, so I ready myself to say a few words to the attendees. But I can't concentrate while reading the words I had intended to say. I knew my father cheated on my mother, even before she did. I saw him outside his office building with this woman who was not my mother peeling off of him. My heart should have fallen out then, but because I loved my father so much, not even this was wrong. It was like looking at my parents in their youth—two bodies clanging. Love, to me, had always been something more than just two bodies in love. The history of it. The mythic history. That's what mattered to me.

I get up and take another look at the picture of Julia's coffin. Staring at all the people, what I notice now is the distance. The gap between these mourners and Julia.

If Julia had been an ordinary woman, a woman who was not a poet but had just remained in her rural Carolina, she would have been deemed "loose," would have been vilified in her society. Men would have turned the other way and women would not have recognized her as one of their own. But because she was a poet, a talented woman, she could never, ever again be ordinary or held to traditional ideas once she had written a few verses. But what about the common people? Is there no cleansing for them? No redemption? The love of these mourners is pure, magnanimous, and forgiving only because they love her at a distance.

But this is not the way we really love, not the way my mother could ever love my father. Love between two people is up close, disheveled—a mélange of past, present, future love and acrimony. And this is how I must love my mother. Love her the way I want her to love my father again.

♥

"In closing, I want to express my great respect for academics. Everyone gives praise to people who work in the nonprofit sector or were lawyers, like my father, who fought for someone's rights, or to poets—they get many accolades. We have dedicated this evening to a poet, but I want to tell you tonight that without academics, the writer cannot exist. It is a symbiotic relationship. Generation to generation, who will remember Julia? My father was the one who taught me about Julia, but what if he had not been around? He is just one man. Who will know her if you do not go into your classrooms each semester and teach the poetry of Julia de Burgos?

"There is a great amount of work that academics do. They remember people, they resurrect long-forgotten reputations, they restore people to their place in history. And they commemorate everything; they can see the writer in all her failings and also appreciate her moments of glory. My mother is an academic, and I want to dedicate this evening and exhibition to her. Thank you."

I tumble off the stage and look for my mother. I have spent my life holding on to my father. She finds me first and gives me a hug. And I hold on to her.

♥

"Of course," Maceo murmurs into my ear when I ask him to dance. I feel the solidity of him when I put my hand on his shoulder and he takes my right hand in his. We dance by the picture of Julia and Grullón in New York. She sits in a chair, dressed in black, with haughty pearls fit for a doctor's wife around her neck. Grullón, dressed in gray, stands behind her. I know on this night he took her out with his bourgeois friends. But the focus of the photo is so tight that Jose assumed that Grullón's hands were in his pockets. That tells one story. But if his hands were on the small of her back—that tells another. And if Mr. Jack Agüeros had told the story of Julia and this evening out with Grullón, he would tell of the focus on her and of Grullón leaning into the photo like an afterthought. But if my father told the story. If my mother told the story. If I told the story . . .

SUMMER OF NENE

I was there when he fell. We were fucking around in Central Park. Had been smacking girls on their asses and running away. Then one started yelling real loud and this cop appeared out of nowhere so we just started running. Nene was behind me, he was always smaller, more frail—that cat was always sick, ever since he was a little kid, there was always some shit wrong with him. So I'm just jettin', but I always used to look over my shoulder for him. That was a habit. But this time I heard him scream before I looked, and I saw my man tumble over some rocks. And I imagined the rocks pierced his back, and he's stuck there for life. Me and the cop got to him at the same time, and my instinct was just to grab him, but this cop dude was like, "No, you should leave him where he is, you'll hurt him more." But everything in me was fighting to pull him up. He looked all fucked up, like someone dropped Humpty Dumpty, and I wanted to put him back together. Set everything right, so he's whole again. Nene was always strong, I mean he was always sick, but you know he was always down to go outside and terrorize the neighborhood with us. And he would play with that sick shit too. See, everyone on the block knew about his illnesses, hospitalizations, etc., and no matter what he'd done the previous day, they always let the shit go. So sometimes I would have to leave him where he was because he wasn't going to catch it, but my ass would.

♥

It didn't even start with him sucking my dick. No foreplay shit like that. I watch movies and it always starts like that, the inevitable creep to the dick. Nene was sleeping over at my house, and it was finally quiet at three in the morning, and that's when he starts. I have my back to him with nothing but my underwear on, and then I feel it next to me, on my skin. Right up against my ass. Then he's pushing harder, trying to find the hole. He breaks through, and it's a whole new life.

The next morning he looks run down, coughing all over the place, so my moms takes him home because she's scared I'll get whatever he has. But she doesn't understand that I have never caught what Nene has. But she becomes the concerned mother all of a sudden and takes him away.

♥

After the fall, we are sitting in the hospital waiting. And I cry, but not those tears of sadness, it's the tears of anger. The kind where you can't breathe, my face gets all hot, and I can't hold it in at all. Guttural noises are scattered in with my language. My fists are in a ball, and I just want to hit myself. My mother doesn't understand this rage. If only she would just shut the fuck up and let me cry . . . all she's done is tell me that I have to be strong. But what does strength have to do with love?

He doesn't get out of the hospital for weeks, and when he does, he can't walk anymore. I'm on the stoop, and we see him coming down the street, but Nene doesn't look all sad. For us nothing has changed, so we're just happy to have him home. His mother won't let him come out today though. She says he has to rest in bed first, figure out how to go to the bathroom, shit like that.

The next day, me and Kenny are just waiting and by, like, eleven, he's still not down there. So I stand on the sidewalk and I yell, "Neeeneeee, Neeeneeee," over and over until his moms sticks her head out the window and starts yelling at me. "Don't you know he can't walk? Get your lazy ass upstairs and knock on the door like a normal person." I laugh and run up because at least I know he can come out and hang with us. He's sitting in his bed when I get there. The lock of hair on his forehead is wet. And I'm like, "My man you need a haircut, you look like John Travolta and shit." His house is mad hot. I pull the covers off of him and his legs look like my sister's, thin and pale. Not me. I'm already brown but this burning summer has me even darker, so if I was sick you wouldn't be able to tell just by looking at me. You can see everything written on this cat's face. On his body. I pick him up and put him in his chair. Then I wheel him to the bathroom, but I make the ride fun, I'm crashing into the wall, I try to zoom here and there, but, in reality, his apartment is too small for that. I call his mother to shower him. I'd be scared to undress him, to see him naked. I always have my back to him, and it's always a surprise. I expect it whenever he's at my house, but I can't tell you the precise moment, only that it's after the house is quiet. I tell her I'll be downstairs waiting for him. She's like, "You better not fuck around, I need you to come back up here and carry Nene down."

I go downstairs and have all this energy, but all I can do is wait for Nene. Kenny sits on the stoop, but I'm on the sidewalk, walking from here to there, the length of the stairs, and I'm telling him a story real loud. Then Jessica, this girl in my eighth-grade class who has the fattest ass, walks by. And she's like, "Hey Jimmy, what's up?" Then Kenny perks up. She stands in front of me and the way she moves from side to side, I know she's showing off for me, and I give her that papi smile. In that instant, I've moved from boy to man. I think of her under me. I know who I'm supposed to be. With Nene though, I know who I am. She starts laughing at whatever shit I tell her, and she glitters in the sun. Midlaugh—hers—Nene appears. His stepfather brought him down and barks at me to get his wheelchair. He leaves Nene at the bottom of the stoop, and I run upstairs. When I get back, I've forgotten all about Jessica.

♥

I never realized how important words are until I see them fight. I scrutinize them to see what it's like to be in a real grown-up relationship. They spend all their time in front of the TV now. No giggles coming from her bedroom. No desire to be together, alone with their love. When I come in, I sit in the living room with them because if they are going to get live, they'll do it with me there. It won't matter. What they have to say to each other is much more important. I've never seen so much of my mother before this summer, so much of her emotions. Sure, she's beefed with her other boyfriends, but I've never paid attention before. It held no interest for me. In the middle of their yelling, I look at the picture of them next to the TV. They're at a picnic, and he's hugging her from behind. The way they argue though it's like the fights you see on TV. It's like they don't have their own words. She says things like, "How can you do this to me?" and "Don't you love me anymore?" Her speech may not be real, but I know her pain is. Even if her reaction is straight out of a soap opera.

I can see the arteries in her heart choking her. The way she can barely breathe and the tears streaming down her face. Cutting off her breath.

It almost breaks my heart.

He says things I've heard before too: "You make me do this. You're overreacting. I don't know what you're talking about."

I can almost mouth along and anticipate what their next words will be. And it's the same fight every few days. This time, though, she punches the wall and leaves. He does nothing that I don't expect: he doesn't cry, he doesn't sit in a chair and try to talk to me about it. Nothing. He does what he is supposed to do. He swears at the slammed door. And takes off a few minutes later saying he doesn't need this shit. Then there is silence.

♥

In the middle of the summer, Kenny's mother goes to PR, and the first night she's gone, he invites me, Nene, and a few females over. As soon as the girls get there, I start to get nervous. We sit on the living room floor and play spin the bottle. But the chick gets to decide where she's going to kiss the guy. Jessica spins first and she gets Kenny and kisses him on the cheek. Rebecca spins next and she gets Nene; she giggles nervously, stands up, and kisses him on the cheek. But when Jessica spins again, she gets me, and she takes me into Kenny's mom's room and just keeps kissing and kissing me on the mouth. We both come out cheesing because everyone is staring at us. I eye Nene, but he looks beyond us.

As soon as the girls leave, Kenny turns to me and asks me what happened with Jessica.

"Naw, nothing really happened. It was no big deal."

"Yeah, tell us what happened," Nene chimes in before he turns around and goes down the hall to the bathroom.

"No big deal? Is that why you had that Kool-Aid smile on your face? Come on man, tell us what happened. Did you touch her titties? Anything?"

"Naw, she was talking at first waiting for me to kiss her, then she must've got tired of waiting and kissed me. She's cute, but you know, I'm not really feeling her."

"Nigga, are you gay? What's not to like? That bitch is fine."

By the time Nene returns, Kenny has moved on and is telling me about him and Rebecca.

We never speak about what we do. Our words come in the form of knots in our hearts, glances, and brief touches on the hot of my back. After the girls go home, we all go into Kenny's room to sleep. He has two twin beds, and Nene and I crawl into one of them. I know he won't touch me tonight because Kenny is here, but I can't sleep. He's so close to me. And I don't think he will understand about Jessica. That there is no desire there. It's not so much mechanical, but I love the fact that I can touch her in front of so many people. The flaunting of it. And when I let her kiss me, I think of Nene. That he could sit across from me, spin bottles, and that we could kiss in front of two, three, six people. He's asleep and his breath is against my neck, and it warms my entire body. I push against him, so I can feel the part of his lips on my back. And maybe this is as public as we can get.

♥

It has to be the hottest day we've had all summer. But, of course, we say that every day. The little girls across the street have been running back and forth to the bodega all morning, sucking on Icees and limbers. Kenny and I are too uncomfortable to even talk. We've been waiting for Nene to come down for, like, at least half an hour, but in this heat it seems like two. I lie back on the step and squint up at the sun and wonder how the fuck it can be so blazing. When Nene gets downstairs, he's pale as shit, and I'm like, how come this dude doesn't get any darker in the summer. It's hot out here.

"Damn, I just found out I have to go to Wilson High this year," Nene says when his stepfather leaves.

This comes as a blow because for the past few days we'd been making plans for how we were going to take care of Nene during the school year. How we were going to take turns picking him up in the morning and taking him to school, carrying his books, and shit like that.

"Why?" Kenny and I ask.

"Richmond High says they can't accommodate students in wheelchairs. This sucks man, can't do shit because of this wheelchair. Everything is getting all fucked up."

Kenny and I don't say anything to that. We can see that Nene is about to cry. This is the only time we've seen him get upset about the wheelchair.

"Damn, and that's a tech school, what are you gonna do there?" Kenny asks.

"I don't know, man. I don't think I even know someone who goes there."

"Yeah, me neither."

We sit in silence, and behind my sunglasses I watch Nene. He's sweating a lot. The back of his legs stick to the cloth of his seat. The sun makes it unbearable to just be in my shorts, so I can imagine how miserable he must be now.

"Man, it's too hot to be out here, I'm going back in. Jimmy, take me upstairs. I'll see you guys later," Nene says.

"Naw, man, don't go. We can go to my house and chill in the AC or we can go somewhere," I say.

"No, I'm just going to get back in bed," Nene says. "I'll find you guys later."

Kenny and I eventually make it over to his house instead. We lie under the AC, even though his mother will kill him if the bill is too high when she gets back, and watch TV until Kenny asks me how long I think Nene can make it.

For once I allow myself to take the question seriously: "He's always been sick. You weren't there when he transferred into our third-grade class. He fainted the first day, but then he came in the next day and punched this kid who had laughed at him in the face. He's a tough little fucker, but I don't know, man. This summer has been worse than usual, but that's probably just because of the accident."

When I had taken him upstairs, he had his arms around my neck and for the first time ever he kissed me. It's the same way with the sex, he rushes in, no soft kisses, but insistent and throbbing. And when he pulls away— because it's always him pulling away—I feel sapped and like my world isn't the same; it's depleted. He takes my strength from me, but it's just to take, because he never gets stronger.

♥

Jessica stands above me and dares me to kiss her. Kenny leans against a car and smirks at me. She's wearing a tank top, and I can see that she's not wearing a bra. She has long legs that are barely covered by her tiny black shorts. She's fine, and I can see how pretty she will be in the years to come. I lean back and lick my lips. I tell her to come here, and when she leans in, I kiss her. I taste every corner of her mouth, and I think about TV and how people fall in love, have families, and spend lives together. Not like it is around here; people love for a little while. My mother's last boyfriend was around for a year, but before that she had had boyfriends here and there. And I wonder what makes love last.

♥

All week I've been waiting for his mother and stepfather to leave for the DR for a week. She asked if I could stay with Nene. I got my moms to agree real quick. I've been fantasizing about how we can act like a married couple. Watch videos in bed. Eat cereal when we want or just whatever we like. Nene's mother said she was going to leave money and food in the refrigerator for us. I take a shower before I get there and try to look a little nicer than I have all summer. I knock on the door and my heart is thumping. I thought about buying him flowers or something, but I didn't know how that would look or how he would feel about that so I just show up empty-handed. He opens the door, and I smile at him like I do at Jessica. He acts pissed and turns and goes into the living room.

"Hey, what's wrong, man?"

"Nothing, man."

"Oh." I reach out to smooth his hair that is flopping down on his forehead, so he won't be hot, but he mad grills me. I take my hand away and think about what could be bugging him. Kenny probably told him about Jessica. "Yo, man, aren't you excited that we're going to spend all this time together?"

I'm not sure if I should proceed because we never

talk about what goes on between us. But I will burst if I sit here and don't say anything. I've been looking forward to being alone with him, just so we can have this one week, even if it's the only one that we'll ever have together. So I gather the courage. I march over to his chair and pick him up. He doesn't say anything. In his room, I lay him on his bed, and he tries to look away. I take off his shirt and kiss him on his neck. I pull down his shorts and rub my hands over his legs. I work my way up and down with my tongue. I finally put him in my mouth, and he quivers and quivers under me until he can't move anymore.

In the middle of the night, he wakes me up and asks if it's true, if it's true about Jessica.

"What is?" I mumble.

"I've seen her checking for you. She's always asking Kenny where you're at."

"You know she likes me. Especially from Kenny's party. I don't like her. I kissed her another time other than that but that's only because Kenny was there."

"So why kiss her then?"

I explain that she comes looking for me. Usually I can keep from doing anything with her, but sometimes she persists.

He lies on his back and whispers, "That's not a really good reason. You kiss her because you like her, or you don't kiss her because you don't like her."

I stay quiet. Our silence and the air conditioner are the only sounds that hang between us. He's right and he's wrong. I turn over the inevitable, that this summer will come to an end, and in next year's school hallways there will be no Nene, and Jessica will surround me at every turn. I watch him sleep, and at least I know that this will never deteriorate like my mother's relationships; we'll only be left with the pretty hum of this love. And the last thing that we won't remember is the slamming of doors.

♥

The next day when I bring Nene outside to meet Kenny, he shivers in my arms. The sun melds us together as we stick to each other. And all I can do is look at him in public, this one time, no back to his, his breath on the front of my neck. I'll never have the words. I think that's better—they could destroy, never tell what's in the heart, something close, but they could trap the wrong sentiment, the wrong *what* I was trying to get at and Nene would get stuck there. Under my arms, he stops moving, and both our hot hearts are sticking to the hot concrete.

A radio turns on on the first floor, Kenny starts to talk about what we should do, the gypsy cabs start honking, a lady is yelling at her man. The world wakes up.

SOME SPRINGS GIRLS DO DIE

"I am going to die today," she must've said as she leaned over to turn off her alarm, pulled herself up, and studied herself in the mirror knowing that this was the last morning of her life. Her final shower, the last time she would brush her teeth, wash her hair. And all these actions must've felt like the first time because she knew they would never occur again.

♥

I wake up before him and go to my 7:30 a.m. aerobics class. I feel energized, like I can scale mountains by virtue of him lying in my bed. Days without him, and there are many, are not the same. I must mirror her sometimes: sullen and on the edge. But not today. For once, I can follow the routine. I kick my legs up high.

When I reenter my room, I stare at him sleep with his mouth slightly open.

I want to run my fingers over his skin because he is always so hot and I am always so cold, press my lips against his so that he'll open those apple-green eyes that I so dearly want to pluck. Crawl inside him, so we'll never be apart.

But I just observe.

And when he opens his eyes, it is to watch me undress.

♥

The rudimentary elements of my day remain unchanged—work, classes, the same things I've done all semester—but he is here today and that makes all the difference in the world. I am dancing: turning, turning, turning.

Her steps must've been light today. Death always seems to come heavy in the night, but it awoke her with a kiss this morning. And surely he was all that she saw before her vivid brown eyes.

My outfit is exceptional because of him. A light-blue tank top that only reveals so much because what I really want to say is "See here, I am lovely to behold." But words so truth-bearing do not pass my lips.

She must have worn delicate spring colors on her last day of life. Gone to work and classes. Done the things she had carried out all semester long, but today was memorable. And that made all the difference in the world.

But that seems wasteful. What would I do if I knew that at some point in the day I was going to take my own life? I would go to Central Park, or even the steps of Low Library, let the spring sun penetrate and warm me all over. Remembering all that was bottled inside, I would instead let these revelatory letters fly into the wind in exchange for hearing my laugh resonate throughout the campus. Hear my voice one last time.

But no. Today was too cold, so she couldn't have gone, I wouldn't have gone to the steps or Central Park. I think I would have simply said goodbye, given people the chance to later imagine the things they would regret not saying.

She must've passed some of her friends on campus, said hello, and parted as if tomorrow were another day. I might have whooshed by her on my way back to my room, and she, knowing what I was rushing back to must've turned away, letting her hello absorb into the ground, knowing we were heading in the same direction. And what about the ones she didn't turn away from? Did she wrap Cathy in a hug? Did she mirthfully laugh and bitch about our take-home exam for Soto's class, proclaiming that she didn't know how she'd ever get it done?

She must've cleaned her room. Put on new underwear. Perhaps she considered all the times hands touched her panties, how indistinguishable they all were. She must've remembered well those who battered her heart. Those who made her feel that the stretchmarks on her arms were not fit to be seen. She must've reminded herself of the sorrows of life, made a catalog, gone down each one. Pulled out all the atrocities that assured her her life was a tragedy.

♥

I return to my room in the afternoon to find him asleep again. He's cleaned my room and I laugh because I don't recognize it as my own. When I close the door it's just me and him in this world, and it brings me delight that he is my little prisoner. And I begin that long journey to reach him. I worry about how I look and if I can satisfy him with this body of mine. I consider hope— my hope that sustains us, keeps us bound. How I wish words could change him, open his heart in two, some for me.

But as always, all I end up with is his hot skin at my

fingertips when what I really want is to enter him and touch the skin beneath the skin.

His words smack me and pummel my heart. When I ask for a relationship, he shakes his head and raises his voice. I know he loathes me and if he were a different kind of man, he would use his fists instead of his words, and the rejection seeps in through the fissures he has created. But before he leaves, it is the same as every other time: we make up in hurried kisses, as if our lives depended on them.

His too.

She must have felt like I do today, disembodied, with a continual squeeze in her chest. For me, because of his presence but absence, and how he can see right past me but all I can see is him, and how nothing matters, not this degree, not my "bright future," and how neither one of us focuses on me but rather on his future or his impending departure that surely must play somewhere behind me.

And when he leaves, I am left with the ordinariness of my life.

Only later, when I am alone, do I wonder what I had been doing at the moment of her death. Was I breathing hard into his ear? Fingers pressing into his back as if Bernini had sculpted us? Me, more Hades than Persephone. Was I going down on him? His cock in my mouth and me thinking the seasons could come and go and there would be no better place for me?

But in that instant, with the news still in my ears, I just wanted to wrap my legs around him. Arms twisting around his neck like one thousand ropes. A girl, ready to die.

THE BELINDAS

It is in the middle of my third week working at Columbia Law School's career services office when he finally comes in. I'm standing in front of the brown filing cabinet—the one that has a dent in the top right corner because a law student flipped out a few years ago and threw one of those heavy-ass case law books at it—and I smell his cologne. Obsession. And when I turn around, there he is. David.

My heart remains flatlined; my anger, like his, is private. I had made half-hearted attempts to find him. Vanessa, my old college roommate, told me he had transferred to Columbia as an L2. When we were undergrads here, I was pleased that he hadn't been accepted into a first-tier law school. Things would not be well for him either. I walked around campus hoping to spot him, but I knew sooner or later he'd have to come in here. He stands in front of me now, and all I want to do is catalog how much he's changed.

Or. Or, remained the same.

He is five foot eight, light-skinned, and stocky. He's wearing J.Crew khakis, a striped blue-and-white shirt from Brooks Brothers that he probably got on sale, and a navy peacoat. Like everything else about him, he dresses for the man he thinks he should be, not for the man he is. He no longer has the fade he had in college or the goatee. The scar over his left eyebrow is barely discernible. His fingers are still stubby, but his nails are now clipped, clean, and I imagine he has spent his morning rubbing lotion into his hands. When he first started Columbia as an undergrad, he wore Timbs, wifebeaters, and a small diamond stud in each ear. David is now a law student here, but a year and a half ago we were inseparable. Incredibly, he looks untarnished, he is still very attractive, and I am unrecognizable.

Even though Lala's voice changed when he came into the room—more giggles and uh-huhs—she is clearly on a long call, so David just comes up to my desk. His heart doesn't skip a beat; his thoughts don't fuse two contradictory images. I am begrudgingly pleased that the face I once had has melted away under these layers upon layers of fat.

"I know it's kind of early, but do you know what clinics are going to be offered in the fall?" he asks. His voice remains unchanged. It's the voice that tells you he is from East Harlem, hard and raspy, a voice I imagine won't bode well in Corporate America.

"I want to plan my schedule early because . . ."

I lean forward a bit. Does he really not recognize me?

My heart accelerates because the more he talks, the more I realize my answer cannot be a simple yes or no, and I begin to wish Lala would get off the phone. I always imagined this confrontation, but never past this point. He finishes his questions; I look at Lala. I know he will recognize my voice. I open my mouth wondering if I should attempt to disguise it and shuffle some files around my desk. He stares at my silence; he looks at Lala. I can hear him cracking his knuckles in the pocket of his peacoat, a nervous habit when he is annoyed. Old Belinda reappears and smiles at him. Then the tiniest smirk appears on his face as he steps back and slightly rolls his eyes. Even though that breaks the standoff, I realize he thinks I'm flirting with him. I eye him rudely.

Lala hurries off the phone and eagerly steps up to help him. "Oh, she's new," she says as she points to the stupid "Hi My Name Is" sticker she's had me wear. I touch it, remembering it says "Carmen." I have told everyone to call me by my middle name. I gave them no options; I didn't even mention Belinda.

I lower my head and try to read through the files on my desk, but everything in me is in tune to his movements, his sounds. I feel him looking at me, seeing a large hump of a humiliated girl. Forcing myself not to stare at him, I train my eyes on the student files in front of me instead. I try to focus on the names, on separating the applicants based on if they are going to spend part of their summer doing pro bono work. He unwraps a piece of gum, and I hear him smile when he talks to Lala. He lowers his voice, and I can imagine the brightness in his eyes. His body is masculine, but his eyes are feminine. Sharp brown eyes, outlined with shiny lashes—as if wet with tears—that curl up.

I remember how he used to love me . . .

I shuffle and reshuffle the applications, and when he leaves I mumble something, anything, to Lala and trail behind him.

He treks across College Walk, crosses 116th Street, and waits outside of Ollie's. I follow him to the benches in the median between the downtown and uptown sides of

Broadway, knowing I shouldn't get closer, and I hunker down and watch.

I started calling him five months ago. Some days he'd pick up, but it was rare. When he picked up on his birthday, he sounded like he always did—joyful. There was a crowd of revelers in the background, and I imagined pretty, slim girls and the whole of New York on his side. And it was like after a funeral, how you can't imagine how everyone else can go on with their lives.

But like anything overused, the effects of the calls started to wear off and the shame started to dissipate. I didn't want to forget the pain. That Belinda. Old Belinda could come skipping back and who knew what she would let happen to us. And I thought that if I was around David, if I went back to New York and found him, the shame would come back. Running scared.

The hood of my black North Face jacket tightly sandwiches my face. Unlike most overweight Latinas, I have not decided to sass it up and be big and beautiful; instead, I have chosen the conventional TV look for fat people, big and ugly. It's the look that most suits me. I wear the most nondescript clothing I can find: no-name khaki pants, bland unicolored T-shirts that cascade over the distorted orbs that are now my breasts. I'll never enter Lane Bryant, Ashley Stewart, or a sassy store called Torrid. I butchered my hair last week. Long, sturdy brown hair reduced to boyish strokes. David used to love when I lay on top of him and my hair would fall in his face.

I wanted all traces of hope gone.

David picks up his phone and when an unremarkable Latina gushes by me a few minutes later, I recognize the look of his body when he answered the phone—it was smiling. She might as well squeal and clap her hands when she gets to him. Their newness is evident. They rush toward Ollie's, hand in hand, but then he stops her by the door and gives her a kiss.

She has no body: thin, flat chest, no ass.

My body grieves down my breasts, my hips, my thighs.

Watching her in his arms, I know he could crumple her. She touches his face, and I am sure she's thinking, watching the traffic going down Broadway, that she is part of this moment, that the excitement of New York City is not just relegated to those people in those taxis. She has no reason to envy the passengers. She has what all those people heading downtown are looking for. They, her and David, are part of the world, the wide wider world.

♥

I gain about two pounds a week.

My mother doesn't understand why I came home after college, why I didn't stay in New York, why I seem so unhappy, and ultimately why and how I am gaining so much weight. She works all night, and I have developed a routine. I lay a blanket out on her white couches and spread myself onto the sofa. I note how much space I take up each night. It gives me a sense of power, like I am destroying this person, the one he has created.

I tell my mother it's normal to gain weight after one leaves college. That the weight will be lost once I really start my life. Since I have been home, I've gained fifteen pounds, and she has redecorated the house, put away the pictures of me as a little girl in favor of photos of me when I first entered college—when I was average.

She thinks I don't know what she is doing, but I don't need her reminders. All I think about is the person I used to be. She has so much stacked against me to be disappointed by. Every night I roll in my disappointment.

I go to the CVS down the street when my mother closes the door behind her. I calculate how much money will take me through September, how much I can use to feed myself before there is nothing left. I try to get something new every day, so by the end of the summer, I will have eaten every candy bar that lines the shelves of the CVS in Springfield, Massachusetts. Then I will move on to chips, cookies, and hard candy. I like the order of it all. These nights alone on the couch, feeding myself, I know I am safe. My life is in my hands.

♥

I squeeze into a seat in the back of the room as inconspicuously as possible. Every time I think that, I want to laugh, because let's be real. But, as I have learned over the past year and a half, the bigger I become, the more invisible I am. In public spaces, people's eyes usually slide off me.

I'm sitting in David's third class of the day which is hopefully the last. At least sitting in his class beats all the time I had to wait for him at the gym this morning. I half jumped out of bed at 6:00 a.m. and spent about half an hour trying to figure out what to wear. That was probably the most time I've spent on my wardrobe since graduating college. I decided on all black, though it would be daytime. I pulled on some black sweatpants over long johns, a loose black hoodie, and my black North Face. I squeezed the hood around my face as much as I could, so you could see as little of me as possible. Then, before heading outside, I left a sleepy/sick voicemail for Lala.

In each class, he's raised his hand, made himself visible, challenged the professor, and kept on and on when the professors tried to shut him down. My eyes are sore from all the rolling. I can only gauge how well he does by the counterarguments, his professors' responses, and, actually, by how pleased he seems with himself. I had hoped that this was the place where his overreaching would be exposed, but no, here he excels. Nothing has gotten in the way of where he invariably sees himself: always shining, always in the future. Fairness rises up like a soap bubble and promptly pops.

As this class winds down, I jot down his schedule and all the dos and don'ts of stalking I've learned today. NO LONG JOHNS!!!! I write in capital letters.

Almost two years ago, when I was an undergrad at Columbia, I interviewed at places like Goldman Sachs, Salomon Brothers, Smith Barney; but after graduation that wasn't a life I could face. All I could do was stay at the bottom of the pool. Glug glug.

When the class is over, I scramble outside and wait for him and his friends to pass me on by. All day, I've had to hustle behind him. He walks so fast and the long johns have made me super sweaty, so I am glad the distance is short when they end up at Wien Hall.

His friends encircle him. They wouldn't believe it if I told them who he had been.

I was so much smarter than him in undergrad; there would have been no question as to how well I would have done in grad school. I even did his math homework, at first eagerly and then under the yoke of righteous demands.

They take over the place as soon as they get there. I stand by the entrance to the dining hall, watching David and his friends. My body bisected by the cement wall, so if he looked my way, he'd only see half of me. More students converge on their table.

Stunning, invigorated women.

Bright-future men.

They are gregarious. Loud.

In love with life.

I marvel. How seamless he has transitioned into life.

And I am puzzle pieces scattered on the floor.

I take off my gloves, so that I can feel the greasy heat spread on my hands. Whenever I step into Koronet Pizza, calm begins to descend over me.

Following him is what I needed. He is so unchanged it hurts.

Every day, there has been a new memory, something I had long forgotten, that comes up and taps on my heart and pushes in till it hurts. This terrain, this campus, is a reminder of where, who, and what we used to be. The overall disappointment with my life and the ultimate realization that nothing has turned out like it was supposed to. That everything has been a lie—the guaranteed love, the expectant future, the reputable profession.

When I follow him, I look for the slightest bit of sadness, remorse in his body, actions, or speech, but I have found none of that. But still night after night, I follow him hoping a different evening will garner a different answer.

These moments, walking back home with my food, and those initial bites, remind me so much of love, so much of what I felt with David early on. When I see him, time waits and stops, even though the past is in the present. My mind an inadvertent View-Master clicking through memories on its own. The smell of the pizza floats up my nose, eclipsing all the noise and stench of New York City. When I get home, I lovingly place my food on the coffee table and admire it. Whenever I have gathered so much food around me, sometimes, for a few minutes, I think I don't really need to eat it. Just having it is enough.

On Belinda's world tour of grief, Victor Manuelle stays in rotation on my CD player. Victor Manuelle is the king of lament. I love how he comes off a bit obsessive in his lyrics. A man with a broken heart. A man who can't forget.

Even though I taught for a year in Bernardston, Massachusetts, what dominates in my imagination is this beating heart of pain. Radiating red as I eat and listen to salsa music. The color red after being smacked, after feeling hot with shame. Red is the color I imagine myself. Only after. And for a year and a half. Eating Cheez Doodles and listening to salsa is how I spent over a year of life. People give birth in a year, graduate from college, start new jobs, have anniversaries, while I have just done terrible things to my body.

Vanessa is the friend who has held on the longest and would stay in touch with me after I left New York, after I left my mother's house, and while I was teaching in

Bernardston. My mother too. She persists. Still sends me obesity pamphlets, diabetes info, heart disease warnings. Nurse and all, she still hasn't figured out what my real problem is.

And now, the urgency eating begins, the world falls away, and it's only this food. The cold, sweet taste of the Sunkist. The softness of Hostess donuts. The mix of Snickers and Doritos in my mouth. The snapping of a Kit Kat.

All this food: powerful. I take it all in.

♥

I look up from my number theory textbook and there is David Gonzalez.

He sits down and has the widest smile. "You're Belinda, right?"

"Yes," I say, surprised he knows my name. I look toward the entrance of the room, hoping Vanessa will come back. "What's up?" I say.

He sits down and immediately slides his chair toward me. I try not to look at him, but I smell his cologne and become aware that I'm wearing sweatpants and didn't shower this morning.

"I hear you're a math genius," he says, still grinning at me. Up close, he is as cute as Vanessa had cooed.

I shake my head. "I'm good at it, but no genius."

He tilts his head and leans in. I notice how pretty his eyelashes are. "What's the lowest grade you've ever gotten in a math class?"

My heart picks up the pace the closer he gets and the more he talks. "A minus," I half say, half laugh.

"I think that makes you a genius."

I smile and am convinced he can see the rise and fall of my chest. "Why do you want to know?" I surprise myself by leaning in closer to him.

"I'm no mathematical genius," he says as he puts his hand on my knee. "I think you have something to show me. I'm taking calculus. I can take you to dinner and you could show me something. You like Ollie's?"

"Sure," I say, smiling, nodding my head too much.

I hear the screeching of a chair. I look up and Vanessa has a stupid grin on her face while she makes pretend she's looking at something to the right of us.

He looks at her for two beats and says, "I'd better go." He smacks the side of my thigh and smiles at me.

I try not to stare or be overwhelmed by him as he unfurls in front of me.

A week later, David calls me from downstairs, and when I meet him, the first thing I say is, "Where's your book?"

"Later. I should get to know my tutor first, and you should let me thank you." He smiles at me.

"Okay, I'm cool with that."

We go to Ollie's and have dinner.

"How come we've never hung out before?" he asks me. We're both juniors.

"You've never asked for math help before."

"No, I'm serious."

"I don't really hang out. I usually stay home and study." I shrug.

"You're shy? Is that it?"

"Yeah, kind of."

"I get it."

"Come on, you get it? You're always hanging out. You have a million friends."

"You been watching me?"

"No, but you know, if you're out there, everybody knows your business."

"So you know my business? What do you know about me?"

I shake my head. "Nah, I'm just saying."

"Sure, sure. You probably have my picture all on your wall."

"Shut up."

"Come on, you can tell me the truth."

"Please. I only have time for my math."

"You love me already."

I roll my eyes at him. "Do you say that to all the girls?"

"Just the ones I like."

"Right . . ."

"I noticed you. I just never had the chance."

"Yeah, you were too busy with the other girls on my floor."

"Ah, see, you *have* been watching me."

"No, your business was all out there."

"Who did I date on your floor?"

"I don't know if I would call it dating, but . . . Jennifer . . . Castro."

"Ah, her. Well whatever you heard, JC was a bit of a clinger. Most girls . . . it's easy to get a girl. But you never even looked my way. You don't think I'm cute?" he says, joking.

I say something I would never normally say, but I don't want him to feel bad. "Yes, I think you're cute." I squirm in my seat.

"So, what did you hear about me?" he says all serious now.

My face heats up. I'm not sure if he heard what I said. I take a sip of my soda before I answer. "Didn't hear much. She was smitten and then you were gone. So, I thought you were a dog."

He shrugs his shoulder. "There are always two sides to a story. I would never treat a girl I like the way I treated her. I'll tell you about it in a couple of months," he says, and flashes me the widest smile.

In that instant, I forget all about JC. I'm no relationship genius, most of my relationships fizzle out before they begin. There are girls who don't breathe between boyfriends. I could swim an ocean.

We end up on the steps of Low Library, and we chat until about 2:00 a.m. All that talk solidifies our fate. People pass by and try to engage him but his total attention is focused on me. And it feels like it's just me and him in this world. He sits close and even gives me his jacket.

David starts off some of his stories with, "I've never told anyone this before . . ." My ears perk up, and I smile expectantly. He tells me about how his brother Tony died in a car accident when they were visiting family in Puerto Rico. His brother was three and he was six. He had always felt protective of his little brother and was resentful when his mother got pregnant with his little sister Sussana. "We have an okay relationship, but I just always felt like she was there to replace him. Is that fucked up?"

I shake my head.

"I like that about you. It's easy to talk to you. You know how to listen. It's nice."

I notice that he inches closer to me. I feel flushed when he compliments me and like a little kid, I want to do more of the behavior that pleases him. He is so much bigger than I am.

He grabs my chin, and in front of all the people strolling by the steps, he kisses me. I look at him when he pulls away. I'll never forget the look on his face. He looks at me like I imagine I look at him.

"Do you mind that I kissed you?"

"Not at all," I say, smiling, breathless, proud.

"Why don't you have a boyfriend?" he asks as he grabs my hair and pulls me toward him, so all I see is him.

I don't want to tell him; I don't want him to think I'm not worth all his attention.

"They just weren't serious," I finally say so it makes it seem like it was me that found them wanting.

"Yeah and JC was someone I couldn't take seriously. Not like you," he almost mumbles. I smile and turn away. There's so much inside of me that I want to say.

"Let's go home," he says.

I nod my head. He grabs my hand. Dean, the head of the Black Student Organization, gives him a pound as they pass each other. Daniella, queen bee of the Latina sorority, sees me with him. Vanessa's friends walk by us, and with each there is a nod, a pound, or a "What's up?" And there I am. He is with me.

We go to his room, but his roommate is sleeping.

"I'll get him out if it makes you uncomfortable. I don't want my girl to feel weird."

My ears burn. *My girl.* "I feel bad . . . he's asleep . . ." I stall, hoping he'll say the right words. Though there is nothing that would push me out of this room, I feel like I am so close. Maybe he could be the one to stay.

Instead he says, "We can be quiet. He sleeps like a rock."

"You sure?" I feel the tumbling.

He pulls me to the bed, but my body says the things I cannot. I want so much. All that women are supposed to get. That insular love that makes you think you could spend your life with a man in a solitary room, everyone coveting at your door.

David yanks harder, but I bear down on all my weight and whimper.

David stops. "Hey, I'll wake him up. Okay? It's no big deal. I don't want my pretty girl to feel uncomfortable. Silly, why didn't you say something? Get in bed. I'll kick him out."

I crawl in bed and am thankful for those few seconds by myself. I feel so stupid. Almost crying in front of this guy.

"Sebastian, get up. Hey, man."

Sebastian mumbles. His head lolls to one side. "D, you can't be serious. What? Leave me alone, man."

"I have a girl here. She doesn't want you in the room. Come on, man."

"Don't take forever," Sebastian grumbles as he grabs his blanket and pillow and heads to the couch in their suite.

"Thanks. I'm sorry. I know I'm being stupid," I say, grateful that he came through for me.

He takes off his sneakers and crawls into bed. "Baby, I didn't want you to be uncomfortable. You hear me?"

I nod my head.

"I hope that didn't ruin the night," he says.

I hug him. It was a stain you could overlook. I had been told all my life that this is what I needed. So I tied myself to him, no matter how many times I almost drowned.

♥

"Carmen, you seem so shy. Come on, tell me which one you think is cute." Lala loves to play "Which Law Student Is Cute." She insists on prattling on while I would rather sit here and think about how to finesse my stalking technique. I spend my downtime at work imagining sticky situations and seeing how I can get out of them. I was just fantasizing about what would happen if I followed David and his girlfriend into an elevator. Maybe I would nudge my body into hers, spray my fat-girl funk on her.

"You tell me first." I give Lala my fakest smile. At first, I had ignored her. Why would she even ask me who I thought was cute? Even though we are not friends per se, I have involuntarily turned into Lala's fat office friend because she's one of the few people who doesn't think my weight makes me invisible.

"Brian, Brian. That's the one I think is cute. Pull his file. Come on," she continues.

"Okay, Carmen, I overheard him telling you he's in a frat. If I can guess which one, you have to tell me who you think is cute."

I'm game after she names Brian. "Okay, will do." I figure there's no way that Lala can guess. I mean, she didn't even go to college. I get the file, search his resume, find his frat, snap the folder shut, and smile at Lala. "I'm ready. Go."

When I stalk David, there is a crackling that I had forgotten existed in the world. Before, I just dwelled.

It took me about two weeks to have a solid grasp of his schedule, and by default, I learned some of the new girl-friend's schedule. Even though he is type A (so I know he has a schedule that he follows regularly neatly typed up somewhere), I am inwardly proud that I have been able to find him on this campus; after all this time, if I wanted, he could be within my grasp.

Lala starts to pace around the room. She looks especially pretty today, wearing a red silk blouse and a black pencil skirt. If anyone walked in here, they would guess she was the Ivy Leaguer, not me. She is typical Latina—always pretty, always dressed up.

I stalk the streets, and, while my body is massive, it has a speed to it. I would say almost a grace. In each of its manifestations, I didn't know how to navigate these unfamiliar bodies, but in following David, I have had to take control of it no matter what.

Lala looks like a psychic trying to discern the contents of his file. "He's pretty, he could be a Kappa, but he doesn't seem like a sucio. Q? No, I can't imagine him in a purple G-string. We know he's smart, and he looks it. He looks upstanding. Alpha? Alpha. He's an Alpha. Yeah, I'm sure of it. Okay, check, Carmen. Alpha."

My mouth would hang open if there were anything left in the world to surprise me.

"Alpha. You're right. How'd you guess that?"

"Carmen, I got powers you ain't never seen. I can read people like a motherfucker." Lala hardly swears or uses bad grammar, but she clearly means to assert the veracity of her powers.

"Your turn. Tell me who you think is cute," she continues.

I decide to test her. "There is one, but, you know, I mean, he's cute, really cute."

"Spit it out."

"David . . . David Gonzalez."

"Really? Him?" Lala tilts her head and goes quiet and then shakes her head. "I didn't figure you to like his type. I mean he is fine, but he's dangerously hot. That's too much. A guy like that . . . has you feeling all electric and self-conscious when he walks in the room, that kind of dude . . . I mean it's too easy . . . his kind can get you to do anything. And this one in particular doesn't seem like he would use his powers for good. Like he came back here last week to ask me about Professor Ramos's clinic and he wanted me to put him in all early. He was saying please, then he was batting those eyelashes at me. I said no and his attitude changed right quick. And then I knew exactly who he was."

What else can you tell me about him? I want to ask. Seeing us, people would expect me to envy Lala every day, but this is the first time I feel what I was expected to. But looking at her, such a pretty girl, such a sure-footed girl, I don't think she could ever understand how he flooded me with love. Filled me up. That love became so real, it muscled its way in, eclipsed everything else, even blocking the truth. The *truth* truth.

♥

"What's up with you?" Vanessa practically snarls at me. "You're taking longer than me to get dressed." She laughs to soothe out her words.

I stop mid–eyelash curl. "I want to look pretty. That's

all." I look at myself in the mirror. It holds my image captive.

"You were always pretty, Belinda. What are you talking about?" She turns to me, and I can tell her words are meant to take me by the shoulders and shake the shit out of me.

"You and my mom always told me I needed to look better. I'm doing that, so what's the problem?"

Vanessa stops pulling dresses from her closet and stares at me. I feel the heat of her glare and a nervousness runs through me.

"You don't even sound like yourself."

"What? I'm doing what you've been harassing me to do for the past three years, so what's the problem?" I stop myself from throwing my eyelash curler on the floor.

Vanessa takes an exaggerated breath in like she is trying to calm herself. She pulls her lips in under her teeth, raises her hand in the air and flicks it. In my neighborhood, a sure-fire sign a girl is about to pull her earrings off and put Vaseline on her face.

I know that's not what she is going to do to me. I've known her for so long, I turn away from her. "I'm sorry. I've just been stressed. I want to look good. That's it."

When my mother calls from downstairs, Vanessa rushes down to sign her in. "I'll get Margie. Just relax," she tosses over her shoulder.

"Thanks," I shout after her. I have to finish getting dressed anyway. I pull out a white dress that has big pink, purple, and red roses etched into it. It has a bold black belt that shows off my small waist.

"Wow, look at you," my mom says when she gets to

my room. "You finally learned that to get a man you need to look good."

My mother thinks that a woman's beauty is everything, that it can dazzle, that it can wrestle, that it can make a man bow down. I am her only child and was always a plain pretty.

In high school, I didn't wear makeup, I didn't dress up, I didn't look like her. She is glamorous—even in her nurse's uniform. She has a Kewpie mouth that is always shaded red, fake eyelashes that look like they are meant to be there. She doesn't think there is any occasion where a woman shouldn't look beautiful. I would roll out of the house in T-shirts and sweatpants. And when I got to college, it was more of the same.

"Yup, you were right," I say half-heartedly.

Vanessa jabs her elbow into my mother's side. Standing next to each other, I always thought they seemed more like mother and daughter. They always got along better, could both admire each other equally, and like my mother, Vanessa had to shepherd me along to be better than I am.

"Where's this David of yours? Is he meeting us here?"

"No, at the West End. Shoot, in a couple of minutes. Let's go. He doesn't like it when I am late."

"A man should always wait for you," my mom says.

"Men wait for *you*," I say. All pretty is not equal. Men turn their heads when they—she and Vanessa—walk in a room; they get drinks bought for them at the West End or wherever. I get the secondary glances, the courtesy smiles meant to ingratiate them with the pretty girl's friend.

"What do you think of him, Vanessa?" my mom asks.

100

"He's cute. Quite the man around campus. And Belinda really likes him."

"You will love him," I assure my mom. "Let's go. He hates waiting."

"And I hate rushing," my mom says as she takes her coat off and goes to the bathroom in our suite.

I'm furious by the time we get to the West End. I walk quickly in front of my mother and she takes her sweet time. David looks confused when he sees me come in by myself. I rush over. "Sorry, my mom was being all slow. I wasn't trying to make you wait."

"It's okay," he says as he kisses my forehead.

"Do you want to sit down?" I ask.

"No, we have to wait for your mom. She can't be that far behind."

"Yeah, yeah, you're right." I stand by the door and see her ready to cross the street.

He rushes to open the door for her and takes her coat. She looks him up and down and smiles her approval. "You didn't tell me how handsome he is, Belinda."

I roll my eyes. "I told you," I say instead of "you probably didn't believe me."

He spends more time talking to her than me as we eat. I keep trying to join the conversation, but the trill of her laugh and the confidence of his cut me off. I lean back in the hard, unforgiving booth. I'm glad she's not spending the night.

When we get our dessert, she asks, "What attracted you to Belinda?" Looking at him and then me, "You two seem so different."

I give her a dirty look she doesn't see.

"True. Belinda's different. Quiet," he adds as he looks at me.

I soften my face though I want to give him the same look.

He leans over and puts his hand over mine. "She loves me, understands me."

"Love?" My mom eyes me, and snaps back to him, "You don't think it's too soon for that? You've been dating a month and a half."

"We feel the same way about each other," he says grinning.

She doesn't grin back. I grip his hand tighter.

The last thing she told me that night was that the whirlwind, the fast love, was all bullshit.

♥

It's an unusually warm winter day and the whole of the student body flocks to the steps. David sits with his girlfriend under Alma Mater, the statue on the Low Library steps. Same spot we used to sit a few years ago. Two red-headed twins sit by them and look at David and his girlfriend with admiration. To be claimed like he claims her. The girlfriend sits on his lap and gives him small kisses around his face and neck. The tenderness he displays has her beaming. He tilts his head down toward her, awaiting her pecks.

When David finally reels her in, he gives her an infinite kiss.

The girlfriend slides off him and sits between his open legs. She nuzzles her head in his thigh and rests there. Her eyes closed, pleased, sure of the crystallization of this moment.

I turn away, looking at them is like staring into the sun. I wonder if he has told her his prepackaged tragedies spilled early and often, hastening you into love. Because what is love if not triumphantly saying, I know him. This scene is a curiosity now—a scene from another life, another Belinda where fat doesn't insulate me/her, taking desire out of the equation.

They both look up at the sky, melded together, his arms wrapped around her neck.

He loves so carelessly.

♥

Lala comes into the office and I expect her to tell me another story about some dude. Lala has dates on any night of the week, and she seems to think it's her duty to tell me about her sex life each postdate morning. She comes over and sits on my desk. Lala is the kind of woman who flirts with anyone. She crosses her legs and leans over, so I can see the tops of her breasts.

"Carmen, you won't believe this. Guess what I will be doing next September?" Her perfectly red matte lips spread into a delicious smile.

I hate prenoon Q&A with Lala. I never have the right answer. But, I always give her one incredible guess. More to amuse myself than anything else.

"You'll be married?" I venture.

"No, Carmen. You're so funny," she says as she slaps my shoulder. "No, girl, I'm gonna be like you. I'm gonna go to Columbia. Well, the School of General Studies. But still." She kicks her little feet forward.

Lala with a dream? This woman who has only talked

about men and good dates. I thought she aspired to nothing more than having a decent job, going home, and having fun.

During orientation as a first-year student, standing in the middle of College Walk, my whole body hummed. Glee hitching me to all the students who were assuredly rushing unrestrained to stunning futures.

Oh, to retrieve yourself in the past, shake yourself like a snow globe, and be in wonderment, sure that only the best of futures is to come.

"Oh, oh, what do you want to study?" I finally say.

"I'm not sure, but I'm thinking sociology or maybe psychology," she says coyly, as if I might find this geeky or something.

"Ah. Cool. Good luck."

When I taught high school in Bernardston to these country white kids, the student in my class who stood out the most was Steven. Lanky and freckle-faced, he wore baggy pants that made him look hood but he had very white-trash long hair. I thought that maybe I had caught him at an in-between stage, and I was glad I was not the only one reproducing herself. I didn't know which was there first, the baggy pants or the long hair, but I was curious to see which would win out. On my calendar, I marked the subtle changes he made every day. I wanted to know the day that he changed, that he made a decisive decision to be one or the other.

It is the end of a Friday afternoon and Fridays are meant for escaping with the promise of whatever or whomever over the next two days. Or even the promise of oneself.

Fridays are meant for stripping off facades. Women

will pull out short skirts and tall heels when they have spent the last five days looking like reined-in versions of themselves. Because people become who they really are at the end of the work week. And who or what will I have to pull out?

♥

As I prepare for another shitty day teaching, Steven walks in. His jeans are tight and he is wearing a white T-shirt. His hair is long and flowy, and I imagine he has taken all morning to comb it out, so it gleams when he comes into my classroom. He sits down and smiles at me. He has always done that. Never gave me a hard time, even though scanning the room I always thought he was the likeliest candidate. For a few moments, I imagine pulling him aside and asking him how he made a choice.

"When did you decide?"

"I'd say this morning, but I think it's been a process in the making."

"Was there anything that made you choose?"

"Yeah, that girl over there. Becky."

I glance over at Becky. She has on black gummy bracelets made blacker by her pale arm.

"She's a quarter Mexican, but she grew up here all her life. I didn't know what she would like. So, I figured I would try both to see."

I look at her again. I hadn't paid much attention to her before. I was so focused on how Steven would change that I missed this quiet girl in the front of the classroom.

She appears unassuming, like she wouldn't know all these efforts were being made on her behalf. But she seems like she would be flattered by all this if she knew. Not in an obsequious way, but sincerely.

"What do you like about her?"

Steven blushes in our imaginary conversation. He too has freckles that dot his face, and moles on his skin. He has gone through this transition, made his choice, but I still didn't think he had found the real him. I could see him scrubbed clean, hair cut off, walking a bit taller in the years to come. But he was on his way. On his way. At least he made a choice.

I go home that night. I don't eat or listen to salsa music for days.

It's so easy to get lost in this world. To forget who you are. I envy Steven's youth, that he's on his way, transitioning, that he had not broken down on the side of the road.

♥

Victor seeps into my heart. He is one of the best-looking men I have ever seen, and I doubt that he goes through as much pain as he sings about. Salsa is filled with heated love songs, music for nights when you just can't quiet your heart. This is not the salsa music you hear in cheesy beer commercials. This is for depressing Saturday nights that have lost their meaning.

I accidentally stab the roof of my mouth with a Dorito. The pain stops me momentarily.

My eyes water, and I press my hand against my cheek as if the pain were there.

Hard, tsunamic waves of anger come rushing at me sometimes. I pull out the list I started keeping in

Bernardston. Every humiliation, every transgression. The love he had for me "was like no other," he said. All those things seem so glaring now, so blinding. I look at her sometimes, my old self, and the gulf between us widens and widens. She is too disgusted with who I have become. She slaps my thighs. Brings the gloom after I feast. Shakes old, slim pictures of her to make me remember. I shut her up, reminding her who she was, what she let happen. Every time Victor's "Devuélveme" comes on my CD player, I hit rewind. Victor wants his ex to return his hands that caressed her, the smile and shine he brought to her face, and everything else he gave. I flatten my tongue against the roof of my mouth for a few seconds and start to eat again. I close my eyes and imagine what that would be like—who would I be if so many things were returned to me?

♥

When the giddiness wears down, and I come up from the intoxicating haze, I realize how boring stalking can be. I've been sitting outside for over an hour waiting for them to come out of the movies. I pull out my old Wharton application. The one I've been carrying for two years. Two years that I've been waiting for brave men to come out of the sky to rescue me like a POW. Just placing my hand on the application conjures up a new life. When I close my eyes, I can clearly see the girl I should have been.

A few days ago, Lala tiptoed over to my desk and asked me what I was doing next year, so she could put in a good word for me with Annie, the office manager who is on maternity leave and Lala is stepping in for.

Some Belinda shook her head and said, "No, I won't be here next year."

Giving me a firm nod, Lala smiled. "Good."

It's the annoyance in the girlfriend's voice that startles me. It is Saturday night, and they come out of the movie theater on 106th and Broadway together. Their bodies look different; they don't sound or feel so new anymore.

"Why are you being such a bitch, Rachel?" he screeches.

"David," she says much lower, clearly hoping he'll match her tone. "Stop. We'll talk about this later."

"I took you to the movies. A movie you wanted to see. So what's the problem?"

"Nothing. Forget it, David. We've had a stressful day. Stop. Please."

I imagine the stony look on his face as I walk behind them. There is silence, and then I notice his balled-up fists and feel the shortness of breath immediately. I pull at the hood of my North Face to get it off of my face some.

"Don't tell me to stop. You stop," he shouts. "I try to make you happy and nothing, nothing makes you happy." His voice booms through the streets as he starts to storm ahead of her.

I scurry my eyes away when she turns around. I feel her quickly looking at me and the guy walking his dog.

She hurries to catch him.

He growls something I can't totally hear. From her back, I see the way she stiffens. But she doesn't walk away, she doesn't cross the street, she just stays next to him in silence for the next ten blocks.

I stop. My body feels so heavy. Sweat streams down my face, and I have to catch my breath. I rustle in my pocket, looking for a tissue, and the best I come up with is a Post-it note and a Snickers bar that I grab like a sword. I take off my gloves so I can pat down my face. Then I force myself to move as there is no way I will be able to run after them.

When we get close to the art library on campus, she rubs his arm and reaches for his hand.

He lets her hand sit in his for a few seconds.

"You aren't being very nice," she says in a cutesy voice.

In a fluid motion, he yanks his hand away and smacks her arm. In the loudest city in the world, we are in the quietest corner and the noise crackles through the night.

Her body is stunned and hesitates for one, two seconds. I know she's confused as she reaches up and puts her hand over her tingling skin.

They stare at each other. I feel my stomach's seasick churn. David picks up his girlfriend after class sometimes. Those moments when he is so sweet to her, when he does things she could brag to her girlfriends about, those are the moments she will cleave to. He covers his face with his hands until the first sob begins and he frees one to pull her forward, his body surrounding her. They both cry, but as each second passes, his cries get louder. His body shakes so much that it shakes her.

Softly, I walk backward. My eyes remain on them.

Then there is an explosion. I splatter on the ground because I miss the steps. The boom of my fall makes a greater noise than his smack. "Owwwwwwwwww," I yell out. I grab my left arm—the site of most of my pain. I rapidly exhale through my mouth. The bruising on my body is immediate. The red bricks pulverize my entire body, but I stay on the ground longer than I should.

♥

My heart is on my face.

David comes back in the room, but I look at the pictures on my wall—they depict my life. There is no photo of this, though. The sting of the slap still splatters across my face. I keep my hand on my cheek to localize the pain. All the rage displayed in his face, in his hands, gone. He is slumped, empty, depleted of all anger. Just like that. Like a faucet turned off and on by careless hands. He kneels in front of me and nuzzles his head toward my stomach. There is no sound in the room because I stopped crying as he moved toward me. His hands touch me, not the same hands of a few minutes ago or even a few hours ago.

"Belinda," he says.

I used to love when he touched me with those hands. But now they sting and make me someone else.

"Belinda, sweetie, I love you. I'm so sorry." His words catch in his throat. Belinda, Belinda has melted down between our fingers.

"I love you, I love you," he keeps saying.

Even though my face is covered, my protective hand on my cheek, the pain runs through me. This pain and my body meet and bend me at their will. A silent reel begins to play in my head. There is a girl, smashed, imploding. There is stop, start. There is before. There is after.

Soon his head on my stomach turns into his mouth kissing my belly, his lips crawling upward until he gets up from his kneeling position in front of me, and I have to move so he can lie next to me.

I used to love his hands. They are stubby, almost incomplete. Masculine, chalky, dry hands. But how they held me firm. His kisses, his touch—now surface-level. But how they seal my shame.

"Open your eyes," he says. "I love you. I really do. Do you love me?" I don't want to answer. But he keeps asking, so I nod my head.

"Say it," he says.

I turn my face to the wall. This is *my* hour of grieving. But there is no privacy. I am watching this happen. Two bodies on this bed. I am this girl. Her cries pick up again and are a whisper. Her eyes are closed. She wants to be alone. He lies back down, his hands neatly folded on his stomach, gentle, almost asleep, before he turns to his side and puts his hand on her leg, kisses her back. Soon his hands are fondling her breasts. His insistence grows. He turns her face to his. Doggedly kissing her lips.

He stops kissing me, sits up and says, "You can hit me. Here. Hit me right here." I ponder the offer. Would we be on equal footing again? In number theory there are perfect numbers. A six divided by one, two, three can also be a six added from one, two, three. What divides can also add back to the original whole. I watch my movie instead, and I hit rewind. Untrueness wins out. Let us enter a new world. A world where what has just happened does not exist. My hand slithers toward him. I am no longer this girl. I don't know him, I don't know me. I slide my hand over the cracked shell of his face. It all disappears, falls apart under my touch. My lips part slightly as his inevitably inch toward mine and I kiss him like that night he took me to Ollie's and asked me to be his girlfriend. He seems relieved, like I have forgiven him. He is more shattered than I thought, a man made up of pieces that don't connect. He tries to get on top of me, but I push him away. I get on top of him. As I clap my thighs around him, I try to hold us together.

♥

I followed Rachel for the past week and a half to see if she was stronger than me, stronger than David. But when Rachel lingers outside her dorm, applying lipstick instead of going upstairs, I sit down in the portico across from her dorm. I know to wait too. I know her moves.

In Bernardston, I could review it all. Food can only stuff so much. Each guy, worse than the one before— the boys who pave the path to David. How much I have given away. Little pieces of me. Gifts on the doorsteps of the ungrateful. I only blamed him, but he could not have broken me all on his own. Only cracked things break on the first blow.

When David greets her, their newishness is evident. A happy couple. All over again.

They kiss and desperately press their bodies against each other.

People thought we were so strong. What they didn't know was how insular our world was; it wasn't strength. If we stayed and said, "This is normal. We are normal," it's like it never happened. There was always the opportunity to return to a before.

For several months, the abuse brought us together— tightly gluing two shattered people.

And then he broke up with me.

He said he didn't want to be those people anymore.

Untethered in the world, I called him most days until graduation, waited for him outside of his classroom, his dorm. I didn't know who else we could be.

He is recklessly on repeat, though. Just the boyfriend I knew. Once upon a time. Not blooming at all while I birthed Belindas.

I look down, admiring my spreading thigh. I trace the multiplying grooves carved into my skin, sparked by my dividing. How much it is changing—has changed. I know Rachel will be there until she recoils from who they are because there are no perfect numbers—what divides cannot also add to remake the whole.

As I head toward College Walk, I wish I could extend a strong arm, have her clasp it, fight for her life. The two of them, intertwined, shuttling toward me, toward a known future, is almost like a split screen: after and before or before and after.

And I forgive them for what is about to come.

LA HIJA DE CHANGÓ

"You three are really going?" Caleb asks through a mouthful of broccoli. "What if she chops your titties off?" The rest of the kids around the lunch table bust out laughing.

"Shut up, Caleb. What do you know about Santeria?" I say.

That's the problem with these Whitney School kids, all this education and you'd think they'd be less apt to make stupid-ass comments. Me and Melo are the only ones from Spanish Harlem here, and as much as they sweat us for being from there, it doesn't stop them from lapsing into their privilege. And hanging around them so much, me and Melo sometimes participate. Melo more than me because she enjoys all this rich shit, but every day I have to go home and smack myself back into reality.

My new boyfriend, Anthony, makes fun of me. "Hey, little princess, you want some tea? Is your chauffeur waiting for you?" He goes to public school and is just some guy from around the way. And sometimes I fear that he might look at me in my black sweater with *The Whitney School* scripted in pink over my heart and think that I'll walk down these streets one day and see him as something else, or as nothing at all. Like the ones before him.

Ever since I've been at the Whitney School, I've had

nothing but dating problems. Back in junior high, all a boy had to be was cute and dress nice. Now, I'm looking for a boy who's smart, likes the things I do, and is going to go to college someday. But I don't go out with any guys from the Whitney School. Most of them are white and the few black guys here just seem corny. It's enough that I've made friends and play on the lacrosse team. I'm in my junior year, but at first, it was hard here. Me and Melo didn't even bother trying to make friends with anybody, we figured they would just be stuck up. But then Tania and a couple of other girls in our classes were nice to us a few weeks into our first semester.

Tania, a Park Avenue girl all the way, is making the trek uptown with us today to the botánica. Even though she's Cuban, I know she's never been to East Harlem before, and I'm sure she'll sit here tomorrow during fifth period lunch and regale them with stories of the big bad ghetto. But she wanted to come when she heard where we were going, insisted in fact. She says she has problems too.

I've known Melo since the third grade, and even then boys would turn away from their marbles to sit by her during recess. But now, some boy, Chris, a transfer student, won't give her the time of day so she's bugging out, hence her sojourn with me to the botánica. But to me and the majority of the world, Melo is exquisite through and through. She doesn't realize that she is one of those girls who will never be alone 99 percent of the time. And Tania is vivacious, no matter what; her laughter can be heard across the school cafeteria. In the end, if she doesn't have a boy, she has herself.

And me? I come from a long line of spinsters. Based

on looks, sure we could get a man, but there must be something in our hearts that sends out signals. Like a snake ready to strike. So I have boyfriend after boyfriend. Anybody else would've been branded with a big red S on her school uniform, but my strength emanates so they don't. They find weaker to brand.

In this long line, I want to be the shining star. Different from my mother. I want that pounding of the heart I'm sure somebody promised me when I was young. Some neighbor, male or female; family friend; doctor or nurse—not knowing my family's charred history—must have pulled up my pigtails, considered my open face, and said right into my ear, "Someday some man is going to be lucky." And I took that to mean that I would be lucky too. Symbiosis.

♥

Tania keeps giggling at everything she reads. We try to ignore her even though we have matching uniforms on and it's obvious to anyone that we're together. We should have brought her on Friday, when we can wear whatever we want to school. The moment we've been waiting for, or rather dreading, arrives. She calls me and Melo over from across the store. She also hasn't taken into account that the store is the size of my living room.

"Oh my god. Xaviera! Melonie! Come look at this. It says that to get a man you have to go to the mountains. Take *all* your clothes off. Mix some menstrual blood with rat feces and smear it on yourself!"

The customer at the counter makes a point of rolling her eyes at us. We navigate our way toward Tania, trying not to break the ceramic statues of Jesus and Santa Barbara that seem to follow our every move. We reach Tania and try to remain serious, but as always, she infects us. Lizard tongues for love. Lettuce and hair to get rid of your enemies. Milk and honey to solve your money problems. We giggle and gasp with her until the woman behind the counter, Doña Serrano, finally comes over.

We make fun of women dressed like her in the halls of the Whitney School. Bright blue leggings and an over-sized yellow T-shirt with a company's logo, barely legible: *Alex's Autos. Springfield, MA.* I wonder how many arms have poked out of that shirt to travel here, to a botánica in the middle of Spanish Harlem. 116th and Lexington.

"¿Te puedo ayudar?" she asks.

I understand her, but I pray that this woman speaks English. Even though Tania is from the wrong side of the tracks—me and Melo's code for the rich kids at the Whitney School—she probably speaks Spanish better than all the people living in East Harlem. I step up and say, "We're looking for love spells," even though I know it's probably not right to call them that.

She looks us over and smiles. She reminds me of my grandmother, and not in some superficial way where all old people look alike. She really does look like her. Caramel skin that is still taut but makes you feel like it's wrong, like it would be far more attractive and true to this person's nature if it were crinkled and creased. And she has the same short white afro.

"What kind of spell are you looking for? Do you want him to love you more? Less? Do you want to use him and then throw him away? Do you just want his attention . . . ?" she asks.

"Well I want my boyfriend to stay with me and fall in love," I say. What has happened with every guy I've met since starting at the Whitney School is that we've just had little in common. Like with all the boys before Anthony, things started to go badly between me and him. I try to talk to him about the things that interest me— art, lacrosse—but he doesn't get any of that stuff and he's just stopped trying. The only thing we can agree on is hip hop. We met four months ago at the 116th Street Festival. Melo pointed him out: "That's the one. That's the one you usually like." I laughed, but his look was familiar. Curly black hair, wearing the latest gear. We kept looking at him and his boys until he finally noticed. He brought me an alcapurria and a coke. Anthony was the first boy from my neighborhood to tell me he wanted to go to college since I've been at the Whitney School, so naturally, I swooned.

"But to me you look like una hija de Changó," Doña Serrano fires at me. Then pointing to Melo, "Yemaya." And Tania, "Oshún. You three must be candela."

That's what she called me. La hija de Changó. My grandmother first, now her. I don't know much about Santeria—my mother's keeping her knowledge on the hush hush—but I hope this woman is for real and will show us something.

♥

"So, you're all alive I see. And you, Park Avenue Princess, I guess you didn't get robbed," Caleb says the next day at lunch.

"Caleb, one day I'm going to bring your white ass home with me and drop you in the middle of East Harlem with no cab money to get out," I reply.

Caleb speaks and sprays. He always talks with his mouth full. "Latino boys love me, which is more than I can say for you and Melo. So, I'm sure I can find a way out." He wipes at the ketchup running down his chin. "Anyway, what did you get? How does it work?"

Tania looks at me, so I speak up. After all, my grandmother and my father knew all about Santeria. "First, the woman, Doña Serrano, told us we were daughters of certain orishas. Well, the ones she thinks we are, it's a long process to find out who your orisha is, but we must have had some of their same vibes. My orisha is Changó. He's a warrior and kind of a player."

"Uh-huh," Caleb says, rolling his eyes.

"You asked, Caleb. Then she told us to buy candles and pray to our saints. So we did. But I also bought a book about the history of the religion."

"Okay, but do you think it'll work?"

"Well, when you fall in love with me, Caleb, you can let me know," Tania says, and the rest of us start laughing.

On our way back to class, I think about how far me and Melo have come. I realize how comfortable we are here now. I had never been real sure about Tania before. I had never met a Latina like her, one with money, and she talks just like the white girls at the Whitney School, and she looks white. Me and Melo have been to her house plenty of times, but we've never invited her to ours. Not even yesterday. But now, I'm sure it's something we could do.

♥

I don't know how to build an altar, but I clear off a corner of my desk and place on it a picture of me and Anthony, the candles, and a picture of my mother when she was seventeen. It's black and white so it doesn't capture the prettiness of blue seas and pink houses. She sits on a horse in the middle of Arecibo, the town where she was born in Puerto Rico. There is a car coming toward her in the background, but she smiles for the camera with glorious brown hair at her side. Tía Chucha told me I look just like my mom when she was my age. I love how audacious she is in this picture. It's in my room now because my mother got tired of me always digging through her photos to find it, so she just gave it to me one day. From this picture, I know that she imagined a different life for herself. That even though she may not have had grandiose plans, never dreamed of being somebody important or rich, she didn't imagine for herself the life she has now. She never wears makeup. She never tries to be the pretty girl captured in this photo. When she comes home from work, she sits in the living room and watches TV. Her life revolves around herself. I sometimes come in and watch in silence with her. I like being with her because I think that if I'm present, even if I'm quiet, maybe she can remember, remember how she used to be.

♥

"Changó has three girlfriends—well one is his wife—Oba, Oshún, and Oya," I tell Tania and Melo.

"Yup, that sounds like you," Melo adds.

"Shut up." I've invited them for a sleepover because I was finally able to fix up my room. I've always envied Tania's room. It's like the ones you see in movies. There's a bed skirt, ruffled pillowcases, and an intricate beaded duvet that covers a down comforter. I couldn't afford all that, but I was able to save enough money to buy a bed-in-a-bag set. It's not the same quality, but everything finally matches and it's not a hodgepodge of pilled blankets and thin sheets.

"Three? Does he have a favorite?" Tania asks.

"His favorite is Oya, she's the most like him; she also rules lightning. He's married to Oba, but I think Oshún loves him the most. She's always doing this illmatic shit to get his attention."

"For real? Like what?" Melo asks.

"Well, she got Oba to cut off her ear and serve it in a soup to Changó. Oshún told her it would make Changó stay."

"Daaamnnn. I guess that does sound like you," Melo says to Tania.

"I would never be that mean," Tania says innocently.

"Wait a minute, hold up, Oshún is the goddess of love, right? So why can't she keep Changó?" Melo asks.

I put my index finger up in the air and take a long look at my book, but I can't find an answer to that question.

♥

I am super excited to take Anthony to the Ritzy, our annual fall ball at the Ritz-Carlton. Me and Melo have never gone, but this year we were determined to go, so we saved up all summer long. This is the first time he's seeing my other world. I've told him what people are like at the Whitney School, but there is a big difference in me telling him and him seeing it for himself.

As soon as we sit down, Tania comes over and says, "Quick, what does 'sycophant' mean?"

In unison, me, Melo, Chris, and Caleb say, "Fawner."

"I'm glad everyone has been studying," Tania says.

We are all taking the SATs next month, so that's all we've been talking about at school. Every time we see each other, it's pop-quiz time. I hope Anthony doesn't think it's corny.

"Yeah, too much," Caleb says. "I hate all this pressure. I still have to meet with my Kaplan tutor tomorrow morning. I tried to get out of it, but my parents wouldn't let me."

"Damn, I'm skipping tomorrow. I'll be too sleepy to pay attention. But I feel guilty," Chris says.

"I heard that years ago, the teachers arranged for someone to come to the school the week after the Ritzy to make up for the missed session tomorrow, since so many of us don't go," Melo says.

"I wonder why they don't do that anymore. That'd be super helpful," Tania says.

"Anthony, are you taking the SATs too?" Caleb asks him.

"Not that I know of. Is that a citywide exam? Xaviera's been talking about it, but I just thought it was something ya'll were doing," Anthony says without looking directly at Caleb.

Chris looks down at his plate, Caleb rolls his eyes at Melo, and Tania is trying to hold in her laughter. My face prickles. I don't want to look at him, so I stare at the students dancing to "I Will Always Love You." Oshún *is* the goddess of love and marriage. When a woman wants a man, she consults Oshún. She should buy an image of Oshún in her Catholic form, Our Lady of La Caridad del Cobre. Buy a yellow candle. Place a picture of the man she wants on a small plate and pour honey over it. Oshún has an arsenal of herbs, vegetables, and magic that will always make a man succumb to a woman's desire.

Yet Oshún cannot keep the man she wants.

I find that remarkable.

If she fails herself, what about the rest of us?

♥

"Yeah, well it's like Ms. Kennedy always says, we can't be going out with these boys from around here anymore. I mean, sweetie, at the end of the day you're going to go off to college, hopefully an Ivy League one, and what are you going to do with a guy like Anthony?" Melo says.

Ms. Kennedy is my guidance counselor from the program me and Melo are in. The program gets smart kids from "underprivileged" neighborhoods to go to these rich kids' schools. Ms. Kennedy has been like my academic mother, the one looking out for me in terms of school stuff, but she likes to give me regular mom advice too sometimes. She says that once I get to college, I can meet a boy on my level, and that I shouldn't waste my time with these boys from my neighborhood, that they aren't going anywhere.

"Well, am I going to go out with some white boys, some corny dudes from our school? That's not my style and never will be."

"No, but I think that Ms. Kennedy is right, we'll be changed at the end of this, no matter how much you want things to stay the same. Like, someone like Chris is cool. You know, from here, but at the end of the day will end up in the same place we will. Think about it, when you're thirty and successful, will any of this matter?"

"Yes, yes, it will matter."

"No, Xaviera. No, it won't. You won't even remember Anthony."

♥

I've used studying for the SATs as an excuse to stay away from Anthony. I told him it would just be a few intense weeks where I'd have to be on lockdown. While this is all true, I'm also giving my experimental Santeria time to work. My mother refuses to answer any of my questions about Santeria, and the closest I came to learning about it was when I was thirteen. I begged my mother to send me to Puerto Rico after I got accepted into the Whitney School.

"She *is* older now, but I don't know." I overheard

my mother hesitating on the phone while talking to Tía Chucha in PR.

My tía won her over though.

When I was there, my grandmother, who hadn't seen me since I was six, held me by the shoulders, examined me, and finally said, "Tu eres la hija de Changó. Can't know for sure until we do un asiento, but I am rarely wrong."

"Mai, you're going to scare her, and you know what Elsa said," Tía Chucha cried out.

"What? What does that mean?" I whined. It was clear my tía and my grandmother had big mouths, and I was excited at the prospect of all these family secrets tumbling from them. But with a quickness, they got as tight-lipped as my mother.

I could see the relief on my mother's face when I got back home the following week. She was in a talkative mood as she helped me unpack, so I thought I would try again. "Can I ask you about Abuela being a Santera?"

"You didn't see anything, did you? Chucha told me Mami doesn't do that anymore."

"No, they wouldn't tell me anything. It just slipped out one day."

My mother took a long breath and shook her head. "I just don't like to talk about that."

"Why? Was it scary?"

I let my question sit in the air in the hopes that she would answer it, and a few more after that.

"No, not at all." My mother started to pick at the crusted stains on her sweatshirt. "It just reminds me of what I've lost. I ran away with your father before

I could get initiated, and when I finally had the courage to call Mami she said that I would let our family traditions die and that because your father had been initiated as el hijo de Changó, he'd have all the power and I'd have none."

♥

I wish I had spent more time with my grandmother before she died to see what this gift actually is, to see if I have it. I like imagining that there is this one thing in the world that could set me, us, apart from other families. But it's been cut off, and I wonder how my mother had the power to break away from our family but not from other things. Because it seems to me that loving my father has been the more detrimental choice. Even though she was the one who broke up with him, she's never really left him.

♥

A few weeks after the Ritzy, Anthony takes me to his mother's birthday party so I can meet his family. Everyone is going to be there: his father, his three sisters, and a bunch of cousins. I make sure to look really pretty and be extra nice to his mother. I even say the couple of Spanish words I know to her. Anthony walks me around the room and introduces me to everyone. He seems so glad to have me there, and I think back to the first day we met. He tells everyone how I go to some fancy school, and I like how proud he seems of me. Then his cousin Angela from the Bronx has a stank face before she even meets me. She has on red lipstick, blond highlights in the front of her hair, and weighs at least three hundred pounds. She has gold doorknockers with "Angie" written on them, and I know she's going to be trouble before she even opens her mouth.

"So you're Anthony's new girl," she says.

"Yeah," I respond in my most stank East Harlem voice.

She sucks her teeth at me and is like, "You talk funny. Where you from?"

"I'm from 110th."

"Oh, I thought you might be from Park Ave or something. Why do you sound like a white girl?"

I hate, *hate*, when people tell me I sound like a white girl. This is the moment I always dread. Ever since I started going to the Whitney School, it's like everyone I meet knows I've gone through some life change and this is the inevitable outcome. I try to calm myself down as I'm surrounded by Anthony's family and don't want to be a bitch, but Anthony starts laughing.

"Yup, you do sound like a white girl! I was trying to figure that out this whole time," he says.

"I don't sound like a white girl. I'm just educated." Now that shuts them both up, and they start mad grilling me and I am pissed. I glare at Anthony and feel like an asshole and like he just spit on me all at the same time. I'm not sure which I should feel more. Never before have I pointed out the educational differences between me and Anthony, at least not to him. And now I think that it might be true, what Ms. Kennedy said, that you can never go back, and the moment I walked through the doors of the Whitney School, things would never be the same again.

When I first read that Changó exchanged the power of divination for the power of dance, I thought it was a stupid trade. But I can see it now. Dancing is a way to connect with people, to touch them, a way to find his way back to a gaggle of bodies in unrest, bodies moving and crushing on top of each other. And maybe Changó is just like the rest of us. He wants to be touched amidst all those shifting bodies, and he wants someone to stop and hold him too, and for just a few minutes in time over and over again, he doesn't want to feel so lost.

♥

I walk around the neighborhood by myself for an hour after leaving the party. I stop at Gomez's bodega on the corner where me and Melo used to get our quarter juices and Blow Pops. I pass the corner we would crowd after school when we were in eighth grade, six to nine of us in our black goose-down jackets, loud and claiming this spot as ours. I pass the bus stop I used to go to junior high, taking me to another world even then. I end up by my old elementary school, and through the gates I stare at the front steps. The first place I was ever kissed. I remember how that first kiss felt like a starburst, and nothing has sincerely felt like that since.

I asked Doña Serrano for love. But it was loss. I didn't want to lose one more thing.

My mom comes into my room, clearly my covert crying was too noisy. "Is it about the boy?" she asks. She puts her arm around me and rubs my shoulder.

"Yeah. Sort of." I sniffle, hiccup, and shake.

"Okay, okay," she says. She stands there rubbing my

arm until she stares at my makeshift altar as if it's the first time she recognizes what it actually is. "Is that an . . . ?"

"Why didn't you get initiated?" I ask with needy eyes, and she only pauses for a few seconds while she gazes at my candles, one for Oshún and one for Changó, before she answers.

"Because I wanted your father like Oshún wants Changó. I didn't know if I could be like Oshún, if I could resist using all that power for myself." She sighs and strokes my hair as my body hiccups against hers. This is the wisdom Oshún has over her worshipers. She gives them what they want knowing it will not last. Or that it is imperfect. But whatever Oshún truly desires, she does not want it through magic.

I see Oshún in her abode surrounded by all her magical accoutrements. I witness how she has loved Changó, danced for him, spread honey on his lips. That is how their love is: Changó pauses for Oshún but she continues for him. Yet I see her stop. That is as far as she goes. Oshún does not fail herself; she could do anything to win Changó. Instead she chooses to chase, to tempt only for so long, and lets him walk away because what must be cajoled will never stay and she has never wanted to be the third wife, the third love.

I thought my mother had no power because she didn't get initiated. But like Oshún, she knew that to love is to barter.

THE LIGHT IN THE SKY

"I think there's a UFO," my mom announces with some unease. I gaze up at the sky never having thought of UFOs. It's not a plane because its position is steady; the light in the sky blinks and blinks.

At the last minute, I announced to my mother that I had to go to Puerto Rico, and she, just reaching retirement, quickly agreed. La Parguera is the one place I had to travel to because of its phosphorescent bay. Tour companies run trips for five dollars a person, and on moonless nights, you can see how the water burns bright. I seek to be like the three Johns who came upon La Virgen del Caridad del Cobre while minding their own business fishing in Cuban waters. I am five weeks pregnant and that is the last thing I want; never having been a believer, I wish this time only that a Virgin in any incarnation would materialize and carry off this baby.

I have no inclination toward motherhood. I side with those postpartum mothers who drive their children into the water. Give them over to Yemaya. Let her have them.

My mother hasn't noticed I'm pregnant, and I haven't confessed it. Why speak of things that will never come to fruition? Instead of making an appointment at an abortion clinic, I made travel reservations, booked excursions, and planned an itinerary "to see the wonders of Puerto Rico." Every day I was at home, I said I was going to do something. To make a move, a decision, but the only choice I made was to get on a plane.

The young mother across from us emits her exhaustion. She could be eighteen or she could be twenty-eight. The rest of the boat-trippers revel in their journey to the bay: teenagers are kissing, an older couple lean on each other and are mirthful, and a father and son talk fish and marine life. The young mother rests on the handle of the baby carriage, instead of her three-hundred-pound boyfriend. Even with the baby outside of her, it snuffs the life from her. She is the girl my mother warned me against being all my life—the girl who gets pregnant, retarding her future. When the baby's calls for attention reach a certain pitch, the boyfriend's voice overtakes all of us: "Handle that, Lisa. Damn, no one wants to hear that shit." A scowl spreads on his acne-pocked face.

Lisa's hand droops on the baby's back, shushing it back and forth.

My mother pauses her UFO conspiracy babbling and whispers, "Ueeewww."

I whisper back, "Ummhmmm." He is the man my mother warned me against. As soon as I found out I was pregnant, I broke up with my boyfriend. I didn't want my life to be irrevocably connected to his.

This is a place where a man will build you a house with his bare hands. Every piece of the wall, every piece of the floor that you touch will have been constructed by him. This is the loveliest of reality. When I go into these houses birthed by these men, I wonder what it is like to live your life indoors, tending to the house your man made and the kids your man conceived. I sometimes imagine this as the easier life, doing what you are supposed to do.

But these same wives ask when I will get married, have kids. My answer is never to both. And after each woman whose house I have stepped into has quizzed me with these two perfunctory questions, all have declared, "Good, don't do it." What if someone had warned this young mother sagging with sadness? She would have probably opted to ignore the sage warnings.

My mother tugs on my arm so we can get back to the UFO. "Maybe when we get to the phosphorescent part of the bay there will be a UFO ready to take us away," she says a bit too wide-eyed. This woman sitting next to me is not the one I know on US soil. In Puerto Rico, this elegant woman peels fruit with her bare teeth, picks it off the ground and checks it for edibility—even though it seems like anything she picks up she deems edible—while I cast a wary glance on all the fruit put before me. She recounts every story of UFO sightings in Puerto Rico she has heard despite that, when we were in El Yunque last week—an area known for alien abductions (at least for people incapable of staying on a hiking trail)—there wasn't a UFO in sight. But if some Virgin doesn't come to pick up my baby, maybe the next best thing would be an alien abduction.

A raucous speedboat swerves too close to us, and my mother snaps, "Dios Santo!" clutching her chest as the speedboat's wake makes our rickety boat squirm in the water. "Wooooooo!!!!" the speedboaters hoot and holler as they race away. "You know, this boat was late to pick us up, but there wasn't anyone on the boat when it arrived," she whispers to me. "So, if there wasn't anyone on it, why was it late? What if that speedboat is full of thieves and they're going to kill us all when we stop?" I keep a straight face as my mother says all this because I respect fear. Any other day I would have been exasperated, but tonight she vomits what I cannot expel.

When we finally reach our destination, we are in the midst of black waters, no phosphorescent lights in sight. The captain announces that two crew members will jump into the water on both sides of the boat and swim around to stir up the microorganisms that make the water glow. The men breaststroke and backstroke, creating a shell of blue sparkle around the boat reminiscent of La Virgen de Guadalupe's aureole. I grab my mother's hand, comforted by the illumination of the water. I could lie down here in the middle of the boat and wait for La Virgen's arms to reach up, envelop me, and separate this baby from me.

"It's a blimp put up by the Coast Guard. It's to catch drug dealers coming in from the Dominican Republic," we overhear the captain answer when the father and son ask about the light in the sky.

"Ay qué locura," my mom chuckles shaking her head, the restoration of her self now palpable. This whole time, she channeled my fear, but she didn't really need the implausible.

When I look back at the water, the radiance has dimmed because the swimmers have retreated onboard. Everything fades to black.

One by one, as the lights disappear, only the speedboat remains. I reach for a life jacket. Finally, swimming to be enfolded by miraculous human hands, birthing my own luminescent streak.

LOVE WAR STORIES

Our war—our *love* war—bravely fought against our mothers for the past three years, the war that led my friends to unabashedly fall in love our first year in college and left me waiting for summer break to start fighting again—that war—I know is going to come to a resounding end a week or so after we come home from college, all because the boyfriends quickly start reneging on a thousand pledges made through the course of relationships that started, at most, a mere eight months ago. Ruthie's man writes her from California saying he's dropping out of school and moving to Alaska to work on a fishing boat, and that maybe in another life they can continue where they left off. Alexa's man just stops calling her back. And Yahira. That's the worst one of all. He tells her that every utterance of love, memory created, caress given—stomp on the grapes, suck the juice—all of it's a lie.

Yet, the most important contract broken by the departure of these boys is the one we girls made with each other when we started this war against our mothers: to believe in love. Just the summer before—fighting, yelling, believing—me, Yahira, Alexa, and Ruthie and a host of other girls would tell love stories. And our mothers would tell anti-love stories. And we did this every week in Springdale Park for three years until we went off to college.

This was our war.

And now, love is fighting all of us—it's kicking our asses.

"Maybe they were right," my friends say about our mothers.

"I don't know what to say. I mean, I'm sorry this happened to all of you, but I don't want to give in to what our mothers want," I say.

"Did you even date anyone?" Baby Ruthie counters.

"Yeah, Rosie, you spent this whole year doing what?" Angry Alexa asks.

"How can you know how we feel? We can't believe in this love shit anymore," Yahira, my best friend, says.

Their worlds may be falling apart, but my *worldview* is falling apart. Listening to them, I start to think I *do* know what it's like to be heartbroken. They don't even want to go out there and fight. They're sluggish when we go to our side of the park. Their declarations are muddied, half-hearted, brokenhearted. My friends sometimes seem to linger on our mothers' side of the park before crossing over to ours, and I imagine that if there were a fence between the two groups, my compatriots would leisurely hang on it, heads resting on their hands, and actually listen to our mothers.

Decimated hearts. Blood everywhere. I'm looking at a battlefield full of wounded soldiers.

♥

My mother, along with a long line of conspirators, told us always, "Never trust a man. A man only wants one thing and as soon as he gets it, he'll be gone." The repercussions for falling in love were always the same: a broken heart and a bad-girl rep, at best. At worst, a life of welfare checks and a baby every other year. Our mothers wanted something new for us. But it was really something old. Something borrowed. They wanted marriage. The divine notion of marriage. Our mothers didn't believe in love between men and women anymore, though. They just wanted our future husbands to stay. "Marry," they said, "but don't believe."

The neighborhood women always gathered at my house to preach about how dirty men were. They'd begin by discussing a female literary figure and note how she too had been scorned by men. "And see, don't women come from a long line of rejected people?" Then they'd move on to the neighborhood women, how times hadn't changed. Mr. Rivera, who left his wife for that no-good Ms. Medina, was seen coming out of—you guessed it— Mrs. Torres's house, and now Mr. Torres was out of town visiting "familia," again. Men cannot be trusted. Amen. This was their weekly prayer.

It all started with my mother. The day my father left, all anybody could hear throughout the neighborhood was twenty-six years of marriage shattering. The dishes cracking. Her heart splitting. Everything they had ever been told about love, marriage—all of it broken. And the women started coming one after the other, bringing handkerchiefs, pastries, and their own stories of crushed love. For that one night, their lives held no clear trajectory. No absolute truths. Only emotion, chaos, and open doors.

During the first year of their meetings, all my mother could do was talk about my father. Stories about him were bubbling from her mouth at every meeting. And it was like you could see inside her—the tributaries of memories pumping into her heart and back out. But then one day in the Chicopee Public Library, she came across "Ethan Brand" by Nathaniel Hawthorne (she had taken to going to the library to find out why her husband had left her), and she realized that she didn't have to spend the rest of her years with her heart dangling from her blouse.

I imagine that she came home that night lightly coated with snow, took off her winter coat, studied herself in the mirror, and realized that nobody in her life had *really* told her her husband could leave her. She scanned her bedroom and moved the furniture around. Noticed the dust that had accrued over the years and thought it was easy to wipe away. And placing her bed in the center, she must have reached into a medicine man's suitcase, full of tubes, syringes, cotton, and marble. Lain down and allowed the blood to drain out of her, while the marble poured in. And much like my father the year before, she walked out of her bedroom, unencumbered by a heart.

♥

"Boys? At your age?" My mother glared at me, Yahira, Alexa, and then Ruthie. If I was guilty, so were they. As it turned out, the news for this week was that Yahira's mother caught me getting felt up by Robby Rodriguez in her stairwell.

Three years ago, when we were fifteen, was the first and last time they let us, their daughters, into one of their gatherings. We walked in looking somber, but deep down inside we were giddy. We had been eavesdropping on them since their first meeting when we were twelve, envisioning their expressions as they talked, and I always figured the room looked different each time they went into it, that like a dress, it took on their shape.

"You're old enough to be running around with boys, huh?" My mother's voice was one notch below yelling. I knew she was mad, but she said this all in English, so I knew we, or I, hadn't passed her threshold for anger. "Don't tell me. Don't tell me that's what you really think?" The other mothers shook their heads in unison. "I know you girls live in a more liberal world, a more *American* world." (My mother liked to throw out the A-word whenever she really wanted to insult us.) "But *we* don't.

"Carmencita was the one we compared ourselves to," my mother continued. "If we did this would we be going too far? Is this something Carmencita would do? And if we thought the answer might be yes, no matter how fast the thought came and went, we didn't do it. We were not going to be like her. Clearly, Carmencita was a . . ." I knew my mother wanted to use the word "puta," but she was a coarse prude who would never utter such language. My mother's raspy voice grated on my nerves constantly, but today more so than usual.

Instead of telling us stories about people doing it, or pulling out a story from one of their books, they told us a ghost story. The story of boogeywoman Carmencita. We had all heard versions of the Carmencita story. Her name was the one whispered in back alleys, around campfires, and under the faithful light of slumber partygoers, way after the parents have gone to sleep. As if she's made a pact with our mothers, she comes howling in the middle of the night. Carmencita tells ghoulish bedtime stories

139

of love gone awry. She comes to girls and women who believe in love when they shouldn't. But our mothers offered something new. They said they knew her. When she was alive. So they knew the truth.

My mother pulled out a yellowed newspaper clipping. She passed it around before reading it to us, even though she knew none of us girls could read Spanish very well.

GIRL, 15. STILL MISSING.

May 13, 1955 (Arecibo, PR)—Carmencita Vazquez, the young girl missing for several months, has still not been found. The search has been called off, however, as pieces of her clothing and her shoes washed ashore several weeks ago on Los Negritos beach where she was last seen. Multiple theories abound, including that the girl met a terrible end. The young boys who were with her the last time she was seen alive maintain their innocence. Some speculate the girl has just run away. But, again, none of these can be substantiated. In an interview, the mayor of Arecibo, Guillermo Cardenas, stated, "I remind all citizens of Arecibo that all we can really be sure of is that this young girl has not returned home."

"We saw her at the beach and were probably the last ones to see her alive." My mother uses her lips to point to the other women in the room. "Carmencita came down to the beach with her boyfriend Luis, his older brother who worked in the United States, and two of their cousins from Rio Piedras we had never seen before. Imagine, a girl unchaperoned with one, two, three, four men." My mother throws a look my way. "They stopped and talked to us for a few minutes. Then we didn't see them the rest of the night. The next day there is all this talk that she's missing, can't be found, her mother's worried, thinks Carmencita ran off." My mother paused to inhale/exhale from her cigarette. She did this constantly. Start. Stop. Smoke.

"All kinds of gossip. Screams heard. Nobody knew what where. Sand poured down her mouth. Raped by each boy. Two boys on top of her at once. Beat up like a man. On and on they went. There were so many. Then the worst rumor: Luis had set her up."

My mother said that months after these stories, girls began to hear Carmencita's screams by the beach. She started appearing to women before wedding nights, before third dates, second dates, first dates, and before quinces. She told these women and girls her story and as the years went on, she had so many tales, so much hurt to pass on to other generations of girls.

My mother finished by crushing her cigarette and looking at each of us in the eye.

As girls in elementary school we used to say to each other, "Carmencita's going to get you." It was a game to us. But as we got older, we heard this story less, so we became more concerned that boys *wouldn't* be able to get us, not about some boogeywoman.

"See, if she hadn't been out . . ." one mother began and the rest continued.

". . . with those boys . . ."

"I'm sure they were guilty . . ."

"I had to walk by the boyfriend's house every day. He didn't even seem sorry . . ."

They all talked over each other, forgetting for several minutes—lost in the haze of the past constrictions they were passing on to us—that we were there.

"You remember how fast he was after Migdalia . . ."

"Didn't stop to mourn Carmencita . . ."

"Still lives in Arecibo today. Nothing ever happened to them . . ."

"¡Ve cómo los hombres engañan las mujeres!"

My mother had the windows open, but we sat scrunched in between them, so all I felt was an intense heat. I surveyed the six women in the room—most of them our mothers. They came out in their housedresses, stretch pants, oversized T-shirts, and hair dyed a "Boricua bronze," as we liked to call their particular hair color. Looking at them, spreading in their seats like melted ice cream . . . no wonder our fathers left. I mean at first I was on her side. I really was. But over the past few years, my mother had morphed into someone I could never understand. Didn't want to know.

"But this is what our mothers taught us, and this is what we want you to learn: her boyfriend wasn't just some cualquiera. He was someone we all thought was kind to her. The person who betrayed her was someone she knew, not someone she suspected would hurt her. Of all the rumors we heard, that was the worst one.

Like you, we didn't listen to our mothers. We only paid attention to the first part of the Carmencita story, the sex part, but we didn't heed the love part. Don't ever be that stupid. Don't ever trust a man."

They told us that we must not live like Carmencita, that we should stay away from men (until an appropriate age of course) or they would be the cause of our destruction. Didn't we want to marry in white? Be good girls? Make our mothers happy?

Arrows from under our skirts. Polishing our marble. Warriors scalping hearts. This is what our mothers wanted.

♥

I discerned the looks on my friends' faces after our mothers dismissed us from their meeting. "God, I can't believe them. Telling us that story. I mean, why don't they focus on how fucked up those boys were?" I said.

The girls were mute.

"Why would they blame her? Basically, it was like she was stupid for trusting those boys and then she gets raped and killed. That's not fair," I continued.

I glanced at my friends again. They were still silent.

"I mean, where's the proof that he set her up? She didn't do anything wrong by loving Luis. That could have been any of us."

"I never believed that story, but, I mean, they had a newspaper article. What if Carmencita is for real? I mean, none of us have really been in love, so what if she does come to people who are?" Baby Ruthie asked.

I sighed. "Come on. That's just a legend. Do you believe in the tooth fairy too?"

"Okay, well even if that isn't true, it is true that this girl disappeared. And just think about how our fathers left. What if that's the way they all are? What if that's all we have to look forward to?" Alexa asked.

"Listen, our mothers weren't always like this." I tried to emulate my mother's booming voice as I dramatically strode around the room as we had all seen her do at the height of her fervor. "They were happy once. Things change. I assure you that if they had new boyfriends now, they would feel differently."

I knew their stories, heard them. When I was younger, before the meetings, the newly single or unmarried women clamored around our house and said things like, "I'll die without him, without his love." Because I never saw them flail and expire, I always assumed it was because their relationships had been maintained in some way. By the time I knew people didn't literally die from love, my father left my mother and I saw how she died.

"Just think about how you've felt every time you've even just *liked* a boy. Remember how that feels, then imagine what *love* must be like," I said.

I noticed their faces change, open up a bit to let my ideas in, every love/like sensation they had ever felt came flooding back to them, soaking their resistance, drenching their fear, washing the boogeywoman away.

Seizing the moment, I asked, "What do our mothers want the most?"

Everyone looked around, but no one answered.

"I'm confused. I don't know what they want. Why do they even want us to get married?" Ruthie said.

My sister Betsy, a bored graduate student on break, popped in and said leisurely, "You know, they're traditional, there are still some things they can't shake. I mean it would take a whole other revolution before they get to that point."

I nodded my head, but Betsy kept spitting these random comments at us, some of which we understood and some that we didn't.

"Yeah, and they want us to keep our legs closed," Alexa finally ventured.

"Or they don't want us to get felt up by boys in my hallway," Yahira said, and the girls laughed.

I gave her a dirty look and tried to not join them. "They want us to get married. And today, we will swear we will never get married."

"Are you serious?" Yahira questioned.

"Yeah," Ruthie said, but really asked.

"You're crazy," Alexa said.

Betsy smirked.

I glanced around the room at the faces of the girls who had mothers who believed the same stuff as mine. Did my mother have such a hard time with her cohort of women?

"Well, why don't you explain more, Rosie," Betsy suggested.

"Thank you," I said. "Well, what I mean is that, above all, they want us to get married, but I think instead we should focus on falling in love." The atmosphere changed greatly. With more confidence, I continued, "They want us to marry and not believe, but I think we should believe and not marry."

"That makes sense," Yahira piped in and the rest of the girls nodded in agreement.

♥

We started a war. It was a communal effort. I, along with my friends, went down and wrote poetic verses. It was our offering; we did not want Carmencita to be a hungry ghost for all eternity. Chased by the furies, whipped for eternity for being a whore. No, for being a woman. We took turns reciting our poem each night to all those who would listen. Hoping to recruit others who would not applaud her destruction but who would see the wrong in it. In the poem, we rewrote her story.

The kids gathered around me as I read and the news traveled quickly from porch to porch.

"That Garcia girl is up to it again," they murmured from lip to ear out to the four corners of our world.

But while I stood fighting for human justice, my mother crept up to me. A great silence ensued and I was fooled into believing I had gained the noble art of persuasion.

"Niña, what are you doing!" she bellowed in Spanish.

She loomed over me with her housedress on, hair pulled back into a tight Victorian bun, hands on her hips, absolutely ferocious. She snatched our poem and ripped it into two, four, six, eighty, thirty, forty million, zillion pieces, and it spread in the wind like cremated ashes. She marched me home, but I kept my head up as we walked by the neighborhood women perched on their porches who awaited my appearance. I didn't even bother to look at these women, even though they rumbled, rattled, and hoofed. The fact that they were out there let me know that I had become my mother's equal.

But when we got home, my mother thrashed out her words, letting them bounce off the walls. She would not have this, love is a farce, men do nothing but beat and trample on women and so help her God no daughter of hers was going to turn out to be low-life basura de la calle. So she beat me, telling me all the while that this was the way men would beat me. And for each stroke there was a story. She took me through history, through all the ages telling me about the plight of las mujeres.

In ancient Greece, Penelope waited, weaving for a man who went out into the world and had a helluva time fighting the mighty Cyclopes and the Lestrygonians and shacking up with a different woman in every port. Then there was Julia who lamented over Don Juan, gave up her life, her social standing, all the comforts of the aristocracy, for mere sex. Even the Romantic poet couldn't make this romantic. After all, her only lot in life was to love again and be again undone.

"No more victims," my mother finally whispered.

But the stories kept pouring forth, even through my delirium.

♥

The next day at school, though, I rose in esteem in the eyes of my friends. I felt the shift from harebrained girl to leader. I claimed my place among them, confident I could lead them forward. From then on, it was possible to get them to do anything. And from there, our weekly battles ensued. We read about other revolutionaries: Sor Juana, Erica Jong, Julia de Burgos, Sandra Cisneros, Ché, Fidel, the Black Panthers, the Young Lords. We put on berets, puffed out our hair. Wore leather jackets. Donned sunglasses. We even came up with a ten-point plan to keep us organized. We started a newspaper, passed out leaflets, made up chants, gave speeches, had consciousness-raising sessions with the other girls in our neighborhood, in our schools. We were cohesive, we yelled, we marched, and every Saturday until we went to college, we rallied against our mothers.

At our height, we heard about storms of girls bursting into their mothers' meetings and pouring out into the streets. And even though it was rare for us to meet any of these other girls, we were filled with hope, awe, and bravado that we had been able to accomplish these feats. By the end of it, we became heroes, and surpassed our mothers in stature. Nonetheless, I believe they looked forward to the fighting because we raised their profile. They were able to spread their word because we spread ours.

But now, our war is over.

♥

I wake up surrounded by my friends. I had fallen asleep in my mother's living room.

Yahira has taken my place among the girls. "We want to talk to you," they might as well say in unison.

I'm too tired to fight, plus Alexa has blocked the doorway, so I feebly nod my head. "What's up?" I say in an overly chipper voice.

"We want to tell you our stories."

I want to roll my eyes, but I feel like these furious girls might smack me down. "Fine, tell me your sad, sad tales."

"You know, when Hugo walked out on me, Rosie, for the first time, I felt what your mother felt."

Punch one. The last bit of sleep rolls off of me. "I doubt that. You would compare yourself to that woman?"

"Yeah, I would."

"How can you even say that?"

"Rosie . . . I wish I could explain what it feels like to have someone leave you. It's like someone ripped out your heart. Stomped on it, bruised it all up, and shoved it back into your chest."

"This happened one time, and all of a sudden what we believed in and fought for just disappeared?"

"Yeah, Rosie. Once is enough."

All the girls nod in agreement.

Yahira continues, "For almost a year he told me he loved me. One day, he just changes his story. You're watching marble crack, Rosie. Something you thought was so solid, isn't." Yahira sits down, exhausted.

Ruthie picks up, "Everything, including me—especially me—he drops. And he moves to Alaska. Moved me out of his life so easily." She shakes her head. "And that's probably how your mom felt when your father left."

I stare at Ruthie hard. But I don't say anything. I just listen.

Alexa finishes off, "It's pathetic. I stalk the phone and will him to call, but he doesn't. One day he loved me, the next he won't speak to me, and there is just no way I could ever make sense of that. I feel like I'm banging on this door. I can see him but he just refuses to open. So, I think I know what your mother felt when your father x-ed her out of his life—confused, lonely, like I'm spinning off a cliff."

Yahira then speaks, "We don't expect you to understand, but we wanted to tell you."

"You don't want to hear what I have to say?"

"No, we know what you'll say, and this is not about you anymore. Think about what we said instead."

"No, I'm going to state my piece too. I never said love was easy, but I wanted us to believe in it because I thought it could be a balm on future hurt and make us better people. To be so cold, to be so joyless, to be like our mothers . . . I didn't want us to be them. I mean, no, I wasn't in a relationship, and maybe that's what allowed me to keep believing in love. Maybe you won't always find the love you are looking for in a relationship, so I say, separate those two things. Are they really the same thing?"

"In the end, Rosie, they are the same thing because that is where we get love. So until we find a different mode of loving, love is going to continue to suck." They get up to go, but as they walk by my mother's bookcase, Yahira turns around and delivers her coup de grâce: "We didn't even need a boogeywoman."

♥

"Betsy, can you believe these traitors?" I had tried to talk to my friends again yesterday, but they refused to listen to me. Baby Ruthie called me quixotic. (Me? How did she think she got her name?) Angry Alexa said I didn't know shit about shit. And Yahira said I was Jane Eyre delusional and didn't live in the world that she and the girls lived in. Then. Then, they said that absolutely, under no conditions, would they come out to war, and stomped away.

"Rosie, they're hurt. What do you expect from them?"

"To get up and start fighting again."

"Like they have reason to. Rosie . . . please. The problem is that you don't know how they feel. Maybe you need to go find a boyfriend, have him break your heart, then come back and tell me how you feel."

"Ha. Very funny. How come no one sees my side?"

"Cause as far as everyone is concerned, you're wrong."

"Okay, can you just be a big sister and tell me how I can fix this?"

"Yeah, I have the magic answer. See their side of it. Seriously."

♥

My father. El Malo.

He looks thinner than I remembered, but I haven't seen him too often over the years. He has dishes in the sink and shuffles around the apartment in his house slippers. His black skin that used to be firm now folds on his cheeks. His short brown afro has sporadic gray hairs and he has started smoking again. Something he had always joked that he had given up for my mother and her love. When he sees me looking at his lit cigarette, he reminds me of the time I was eight, and I had pleaded with my uncle to give up smoking the day after someone came to school and told us of its dangers. My father laughs now and tousles my hair like I am eight again.

He starts to reminisce about the old times, even though I am sure he knows why I am here. He tells me about when they first met, and for the first time I can envision my parents as young people. My mother with long hair and long legs in a completely different world. How she snuck out to San Juan to hear El Gran Combo. And how those were the happiest days of their lives and they couldn't be reproduced for all the love in the world.

Then, he sits around and tells me jokes in Spanish that only someone who has spent all their lives in Puerto Rico can understand. And he laughs to himself when he delivers his punch line, and I, in turn, give him a strained smile.

I try to be as patient as I can be, but I finally interrupt him, "Pop, I wanted to talk to you about something. You know we've been having this love war, and now my friends don't want to fight anymore because their boyfriends left them. I figure if I can tell them why, then they'll fight again. And well . . ." I shift in my seat, not sure how to get the last words out.

"And you want to know from me how you leave and stop loving someone?"

I nod my head.

Even though I'm sure he knew this was coming, he has an uncomfortable smile on his face. He's quiet for the first time today. He leans back in his chair and interlaces his fingers behind his head. He exhales and finally says, "That's a tough question. Really tough."

"I know. I didn't come to blame you or anything."

"Well, people think that because you're the one who leaves it's easy for you, but it wasn't easy to leave your mother. I know it's harder for the one who's left, but it wasn't right to stay anymore."

I sit silent for a second waiting for him to continue. "Yeah, but how do you get to that point? You left a woman you were married to for twenty-six years."

"Sometimes, oftentimes, you just stop loving people. That's the truth. But when I loved your mother, I loved her."

"What do you mean?" I try to scramble back up. "How do you just stop loving your wife?"

"It happens over time. One day, one week, one month, one year, I didn't feel the same way."

"Did Mom do something? I mean she must have done something to make you stop loving her."

"I'm sure your mother and her friends tore us apart, said we were this and that, but you're not bad because you don't feel anything anymore. It'd be easy to blame her, like she blamed me, but loving someone or not loving someone doesn't really say anything about who you are as a person, or even if you did a terrible thing."

"But don't you think that if you love a person you love them forever?" At this point, I feel like I am eight again.

"I bet you think love is all you need, huh?" He pauses and takes a deep breath, and is about to continue, but I cut him off.

"Yeah, I mean, if you love somebody, you make it work. Doesn't loving someone mean you do anything to stay together? That your love has some value other than just words." And all of a sudden I feel like I am channeling my mother and asking the questions she would ask. Demanding the things she must know. And I start to wonder what her side of the story is.

He laughs. "Love gets forgotten in daily living. When you are in the middle of a fight, trust me, the last thing on your mind is whether or not you love her. You know, we all say we want love, and we get there, and then one day it's like it doesn't matter, like it never mattered."

"Did you ever really love Mom?" I strangle out. I am aware that my chest is heaving like hers all those years ago.

"Of course I did. Of course. But, Rosie, I don't know

153

if love can possibly last forever, and I don't know if it should have to, but I think you're right in thinking one should try." He pauses and scratches his head. "People make too much of love. Everybody thinks it's all you need, but love is a starting point. There is so much that comes after love, so much that you can't even imagine."

He finishes and glances at me to see if I understand.

I picture him and his buddies, sitting in their living rooms for the past six years, drinking Coronas or Bacardí Limón. They sit around a table and play dominoes and each time they throw a domino down—*smack!*—it is as if they are scattering the past. "I still remember how she looked back in 1963, how I thought I could live off of her smile," my father may say. And he sweats through his guayabera, the one my mother bought from the Cuban man who used to live down the street. Lamenting the loss of these women, maybe they look at each other and judge who has suffered a greater loss and who is stronger for suffering less. Or perhaps they think too that they were told that marriage was forever and never imagined themselves walking out doors.

♥

Last summer, the night before we went off to college, my mother came into my room to help me pack. As I had gotten older, our day-to-day interactions had become stiff. Two rivals in one house. But that night, we laid down our arms. It was a truce. She smoked in my room even though she knew I hated the smell of cigarettes and was super concerned about secondhand smoke. And I chewed gum even though she hated the noise and always said I sounded like a cow. She sat on my bed and watched me place my folded clothes into my suitcase.

"I want you to be careful," she said.

"Be careful of what?"

"Life. Boys."

I smirked. "I think I can handle that. There won't even be any boys at my school." I was going to Smith College.

"There are always boys."

"I suppose so."

"Even if you are not going to be bothered with boys, take care of your friends. Don't be surprised if you need to mend a few broken hearts this year."

"Ha! They'll be fine. We have fought long and hard."

"Yes, you have. You've fought very well." She beamed at me and for a second I thought she was proud of me.

"Anything else?" I asked.

My mother looked up at me and stayed quiet for a few minutes.

"Hija, I have told you everything about love. I have prepared you as best as I could, but you have not accepted it. So how do I advise a daughter who does not listen? What would make you believe me? I could tell you about how I've been hurt but that hasn't shaken your faith; in fact, I think it strengthens it."

I asked her about Carmencita. "Do you think she still comes to those who believe in love?"

My mother chuckled. "I don't know. I know that was really our story, our story for our generation, but for you girls, in this world, I don't know. I don't know if she ever came to girls in Chicopee. But for us, me and my friends, it was a different story."

♥

Anna Karenina, The Color Purple, Medea, The Joy Luck Club, The Odyssey, Madame Bovary, Native Son, The Scarlet Letter. Boogeywoman Carmencita. My father, El Malo. My mother's library plaits together different cultures, different eras. No part of the world is left unscathed, unturned. This is how my mother has made her case.

I sit in my mother's living room—where her and so many of the neighborhood women spent so much time living, breathing, fighting. I remember how this room was normally closed off to us. How it was their gathering place and at one point we held superstitions about coming into this room. It was almost like catching cooties if we touched the door. Even after a year away though, I can still feel the ghosts of all the women suffocating me.

Looking at my mother's bookcase, I no longer focus on the texts. I can only pinpoint which woman in that text has been abandoned, rejected, unloved—all those adjectives for the way women are treated, none of them good. I almost want to eulogize these women. Dearly departed, here lies Anna Karenina, here lies Bessie, here lies Hester Prynne. Women who loved. Women who were wronged. Women dead in books, mere words etched into cotton. How my mother has breathed life into them.

All those years we spent at war, every night, to stave off her life, I lay in bed and listened to the beating of my heart. Sometimes I could not wait to get to bed, to be alone with my heart. It heaved and spread a tingling wonder throughout my body. And it was in those few minutes, with my hand on my heart, that I felt the most absolute delight. And I always wondered how my mother could tell me not to believe, how she could have forgotten that this is how she once felt for my father. I didn't fall in love on purpose this year. I didn't fall in love because I wanted to love love for a little bit longer, hold on to it in ways that the heartbroken cannot. I would visit Yahira at UMass on the weekends, and every time I did, I was always reminded that boys existed in this world too. I met and met boys, sometimes I thought they would catch me, but I continued to cycle past them. All year. Because I worried that if I ended up brokenhearted, I couldn't be here to stand up for love. I almost knew that we would be here this summer. That this would be our new battle. And regardless of how the rest of this summer turns out, I know I am ready for love. But right now, to save my girls, I know what I must do. I climb the steps to go to my mother's room. I am ready to hear a different story.

As my mother finished helping me pack last summer, I asked her, "Whose side do you think Carmencita would pick?"

"Side?"

"In our war."

My mother got up and put the remaining T-shirts into my suitcase, and she didn't look at me when she answered. "I don't think Carmencita would ever pick a side. We never choose one, even if we're sure we have. We move back and forth, always back and forth."

ACKNOWLEDGMENTS

I would like to thank my mother Lucy, sister Vanessa, and bff4eva Anieska for years upon years of support. My mother and sister always championed this statistically unlikely dream and have been excited at every step of this journey. Anieska writes to me every day, multiple times a day, and bakes me holiday treats, and is the bestest friend a woman can have. To my dog, Chocolatte, who makes me most human by making me care for a tiny furry thing with big brown eyes and the cutest black nose; even though she demands her pollito-chicken when I am writing, or she lies on my drafts, letting me know what she thinks of them.

To my writing loves—Racquel Goodison and Kali Fajardo-Anstine: two of the best writers I know, and I can't wait for the world to feast upon their writing. Love to all my Northfield Mount Herman classmates, teachers, and advisors, especially Brad Zervas, Mr. Fleck, Molly Scherm, Louise Schwingel, Geo—for changing my life, Enike, Missy C., Shelley B/Twinnie B, Framp, Squakaroos, Wanda, Joey, and my little boy Ralfy. To my Columbia chums: Maumau, Violeta, Catrell, Tiffany, and Angie. To my hermanas—the Oh So Fly Pi Chis of Latinas Promoviendo Comunidad, Lambda Pi Chi Sorority Incorporated: Adalisse, Tania, Diana, Joanne, Madelyn,

Melo, Luivette, Jessica, Jude, and Rosie. At Emerson thanks to Dewitt Henry, Jessica Treadway, Stanley, and Corrie. Much love to my fellow AmeriCorps VISTAs from Miami who were there when I needed them the most: Dana, CCl, and AEK. At UIC thanks to my dissertation committee members: Eugene Wildman, Suzanne Oboler, Frances Aparicio, and Natasha Barnes, and my chums: David, Nneka, Janice, and Camille.

Thanks to all my coworkers who offered support in a multitude of ways: Sacheen, Jose, Anne, Karen, Jackie, Aida, Joyce, Kelly, Rosario, and Carmen. And then there are all those writers (and editors) who taught me and supported me in ways they didn't need to: Junot Díaz, Angie Cruz, Helena María Viramontes, Cristina García, Laura Pegram, Fred Arroyo, Metta Sáma, Joshua Cohen, Brian Cassity, Jina Ortiz, and Rochelle Spencer.

Thanks to the journals and organizations who supported my work: *Aster(ix)*, the *Bilingual Review*, the *Boston Review*, *Kweli*, *Ragazine*, *Tammy* (Chapbook Series 2), *Quercus Review Press*, *Vandal*, Bread Loaf Writers' Conference, Kimbilio, VONA/Voices of Our Nation Arts Foundation, Las Dos Brujas Writers' Workshop, Summer Literary Seminars, Writers of America Conference, and the New York State Summer Writers Institute. Special shout-out to Authors '18 on Facebook—what a lovely community created by strangers who were on the same journey.

And one million thanks to the readers of the Louise Meriwether First Book Prize and the Feminist Press: Nayomi Munaweera, Melissa R. Sipin, Tayari Jones, Ana Castillo, and anyone else who read. Thank you to

Jennifer Baumgardner for that most amazing call; to Lauren Rosemary Hook for diving in and really helping me strengthen this manuscript, especially the endings; to Alyea Canada for wonderful copyedits, which really do make all the difference in the world; to Suki Boynton, who I am sure has created the most beautiful cover that has ever existed and will ever exist; to Jisu Kim for being a wonderful hype woman—I know a million books get published a year, so the fact that anyone wants to read my book is largely due to your efforts; and to the yet unknown staff members who will take over from here. You all are dream makers!

CREDITS

"El qué dirán" was originally published as "Esperándote" in *Vandal* 1, no.1 (2009): 49–54.

"Holyoke, Mass: An Ethnography" first appeared in the *Boston Review* 32, no. 1 (2007): 39–41.

"The Simple Truth" was published in the *Bilingual Review* 33, no. 1 (2012–2013): 86–94.

"Summer of Nene" was published in the *Boston Review* 30, no. 5 (2005): 53–54.

"The Belindas" is also available in chapbook form as a part of *Tammy*'s Chapbook Series Two.

"La Hija de Changó" first appeared in *Kweli* (Dec. 2009).

"The Light in the Sky" was first published in *Ragazine* (May/June 2010).

"Love War Stories" was originally published as "A Different Story" in *Quercus Review* 10 (2010): 146–59.

The Feminist Press is a nonprofit educational organization founded to amplify feminist voices. FP publishes classic and new writing from around the world, creates cutting-edge programs, and elevates silenced and marginalized voices in order to support personal transformation and social justice for all people.

See our complete list of books at
feministpress.org

FEMINIST PRESS
AT THE CITY UNIVERSITY OF NEW YORK